The Royal Diaries

Eleanor

Crown Jewel of Aquitaine

BY KRISTIANA GREGORY

Scholastic Inc. New York

France,
1136

April 20th, the year of Our Lord 1136
Poitiers

It rains again. I am sitting in the window seat, looking out toward the other end of the palace. I can see Father's knights pace along the battlements. Their helmets look shiny gray in the rain.

There is one knight in particular I hope to glimpse: Clotaire the Strong.

I have tried to lean out the window for a better look, but the opening is too narrow. It is the right size for an archer to stand here and shoot out his arrows, but too small for a thirteen-year-old girl. Only my arm will fit outside. The rain is cold and quickly soaks my sleeve.

Alas . . . Grandmère has seen that I am wet and is calling me over to the fire. She and her ladies are busy with embroidery. To please them I will return to my sewing, but really my interest is to hear the stories they tell one another . . . such drama and romance!

I am grateful for this little diary. Grandmère gave it to me so that I could describe the longings of my heart and my own dramas. She asked one of the monks to sew together scraps of parchment left over from his Scripture copying. When the pages were bound, he painted the edges with gold and then made a cover from rabbit skin. It was beautiful and soft, but in a few days it had fleas. So the monk made a new cover of leather. Etched onto its front is a likeness of me, holding my gyrfalcon on outstretched arm. It is a tall white bird.

An hour later

I have escaped the ladies. A rat the size of a cat ran from a bundle of cloth where it had made a nest. Screams and clatterings of stools tipping over brought servants. They are now spreading clean straw on the floor.

While I have these moments to myself, I want to tell about the jousting tournament and Clotaire the Strong.

His horse charged his opponent at a fierce gallop. Clotaire's lance rammed the other knight in his chest, unseating him. The poor fellow lay in the mud on his back like a turtle. Clotaire dismounted to help him up. There was no blood, for the spear had not pierced the man's suit of chain mail. But by the time his squires pulled off his helmet, his eyes stared up in death. Clotaire carried the

4

knight off the field then tenderly laid him in the grass. When he knelt over him to pray, my heart went soft. I call him "the Strong" because to carry someone dressed in iron leggings and an iron shirt must have been like lifting a wagon.

Some moments later my father, Duke William X, signaled the trumpets to sound, for another joust was beginning. Jesters in jangling hats leaped into somersaults, and the crowd cheered. Two knights mounted their horses and each rode to far ends of the field, to face each other with lances.

It was not the jousting that interested me, but Clotaire the Strong. I watched him lead his horse to the watering trough, his helmet under his arm. From where I sat in the stands, I could see he was more handsome than my father. And young — perhaps sixteen.

Grandmère and her ladies have returned to the fire and are looking over at me from their stools. "What silly little things are you writing about, Eleanor?" one of them called. She is Madame, the chief lady-in-waiting, who makes sure she knows all my business. And the business of others.

I did not answer. The question made me hot. They think me a child, but I am almost fourteen, old enough to be married. They say it is noble to keep a needle in hand, as they do, to weave woolen threads onto linen, but I would rather be like the troubadours. With <u>pen</u> in hand they weave words upon paper. Theirs is a joyous art. To write stories and poems — now that is noble.

My grandfather was William IX, the greatest troubadour who ever lived. He died when I was little, so I don't remember much of him except for his beautiful singing voice. People still recite his poems, but they make women blush. His words were passionate and lusty, Grandmère says, immoral. He was excommunicated by the pope.

My father was also excommunicated. For some reason he hates Pope Innocent II and has expelled the bishop from Poitiers along with the other churchmen. I do not know why Father did this except that he seems to fight with anyone who won't agree with him. When he loses his temper he makes terrible decisions. Now he supports the antipope, who is a Roman cardinal named Anacletus. It is a war within the church because two men want to be pope. Father has taken the unpopular side.

I remember watching from the tower when he drove the religious men out of our village. I was eight years old. He was on horseback waving his sword, riding back and forth along the river as the men ran into the woods. He cursed at them and swore oaths that he would kill any who returned. Father smashed the altar where Bernard the Monk had recently said Mass. I was horrified to see him do such a thing, especially because people believe Bernard is a saint. Since then Father only appoints priests loyal to Anacletus the antipope. This is just one of the reasons many of our vassals have grown to despise our family.

Later, alone at last

Tonight while I undressed for bed I thought of a way to hide this diary. In the hallway outside my chamber stands a tiny suit of chain mail that had belonged to my brother, Willie. It is fitted over a wooden doll. Father had it made when Willie was four years old so that he could pretend he was a knight, but Willie died after wearing it only twice. The helmet is like a cone and lifts off easily with room inside it for a book. It is a perfect hiding place. Even though a torch lights the corridor, I will sneak by when no one is looking. Willie would be pleased because he loved secrets. I miss him.

Madame came in to say good-night. She is married to a knight who serves my father. This is how she is able to hear news and palace gossip. When she leaned over my bed to straighten the cover, her braid fell across her shoulder and brushed my arm.

"The Strong One asks about you, m'lady," she whispered. "He says you are the prettiest flower he's ever seen. Shall I arrange a meeting?"

I whispered, "Yes," knowing Grandmère would be furious if she found out. One day I will be duchess of all these lands and marry a noble. Clotaire is just a villager. Grandmère would say he is not good enough for me.

"Yes," I said again. I could see Madame smile as she lifted the candle to leave. Her dress rustled with her quick steps toward the door.

April 21st

This morning, the feast of Saint Beuno, I was the only one in chapel. It was cold kneeling on the stone floor, and a draft flickered the candles. I looked up at the sound of pigeons high in the rafters. They come and go as they please because the window has no shutters. It is open all the time for light and air. The priest said prayers to Saint Beuno, patron of sick animals. My pets are healthy, but still I asked him to watch over my falcon and the black swans that live in our lake, the many dogs in the village, cats, and horses. . . . Alas, my list was long. Pigeons, too, though they are often roasted for our dinners.

The priest prays in Latin, but I pray in langue d'oc. I am certain God understands my French dialect. I ask Him to forgive my father for fighting with the pope.

Petronilla is sitting beside me now in our window. We are watching the rain. She is such a good sister. Though two years younger than I, she is more clever than all our ladies together. I like to call her Petra. We have just come from an audience with Marcabru, our favorite troubadour. He is one of the many our father the duke patronizes. That means he pays them to practice their joyous art. I asked him to write a song about Clotaire the Strong and said that he must include the words <u>hero</u> and <u>kind</u>.

Alas, my sister revealed her naughtiness when she said he must also use the word <u>lover</u>. Marcabru bowed with a sweep of his hand, then said he would be pleased to do our bidding.

I enjoy my sister. She is pretty, with long braids like mine, reddish blond. We could be twins, for our looks and thoughts are so much alike. In our window she sits with her legs drawn up under the volumes of her skirt. This would bring a scolding if Grandmère saw, for she has taught us to be dignified. Our feet must be on the ground at all times, unless we're on horseback or in bed. But Grandmère is napping, and her ladies are elsewhere this morning. We can sit as we please.

April 22nd

Father has had another episode with the Church.

I was in the kitchen this morning when a cook told our baker what had happened. She heard the news from a blacksmith, who heard it from Madame, who heard it from her husband, who heard it from another knight. He heard it from a messenger who had just ridden from Parthenay. Father has been staying at our château there, collecting the usual pigs and sacks of grain from our vassals. Father Bernard tried to visit Father, after walking many days from his monastery in Champagne. But when he arrived at the château, Father drew bolts across the doors and shouted for him to go away!

After some time Bernard was able to calm Father down, then reason with him. He wanted him to abandon the antipope, for the sake of his immortal soul. At last Father said that he would acknowledge Innocent II as the true pope, but he would never let the expelled priests back into Aquitaine. Why, I do not know. I think Father enjoys being difficult.

There is more to the story. Outside the château is a village square with the church of Notre Dame de la Couldre. The next morning peasants and nobles crowded into the church to hear Father Bernard say Mass. My father was not allowed in, of course, because he had been excommunicated, so he watched through the open doorway. Bernard noticed him standing outside and began walking down the aisle toward him. In a loud voice he challenged Father to humble himself before Christ and to stop treating his subjects with contempt. He urged him to make peace with the bishop of Poitiers, who stood nearby. What happened next is hard to believe.

Father went pale and collapsed on the ground at Bernard's feet. His chevaliers helped him up, but he fell again. When he finally was able to stand on his own, he slowly approached the bishop he had hated so much, to give him the kiss of peace.

Now our palace is full of whisperings. If what people say is true, my father the duke is either faking, or he has had an encounter with God. I want to see him!

April 23rd

The rain has stopped. When sunlight began pouring in through the arrow slits, Petra and I excused ourselves from our Greek lesson to hurry outside. The air was fresh and moist with the sweet scent of apple blossoms. We ran through the walled gate to the river. In the distance we could hear Grandmère calling our names from the court-yard: "Eleanor . . . Petronilla . . . come back!" But we kept running.

When we reached the mossy bank, we climbed our favorite rock. It is high enough that when we lie flat no one on the path below can see us. The view from here is lovely. All around us the fields are green with colorful patches of wildflowers. We could see the peasants working in their vegetable gardens and hauling firewood from the forest beyond. In the middle of all this sits our lovely old palace. Poitiers. Part of the stone wall surrounding it was built in ancient times. Inside there are even taller walls, from which Father's knights keep watch. When they pass by the openings in the ramparts, we can see sunlight glistening off their helmets.

Petra and I stayed here until afternoon, leaning on our elbows then turning to lie on our backs, our braids bunched under our heads for pillows. All the while we watched the clouds and talked about sister things. We kept looking at the road to Parthenay, hoping to see horsemen escorting our father home.

Later

Now we are dressed for dinner, waiting to be called for our entrance. Madame helped us paint our eyelids a light blue and darken our lashes with black charcoal. Like the other ladies, we have pots of rouge for our cheeks and lips. We enjoy using cosmetics, but Grandmère says we are too young. I do not think so. It is the Aquitaine style to look our prettiest.

Petra's gown is emerald, mine blue, and our shoes are white silk beaded with pearls. When we dance we may have to kick out our feet to show them off. The great hall is downstairs, many corridors away from our apartment, and already we can hear music. The merrymaking is to honor Saint George, for today is the feast of Saint George. Once upon a time he saved a king's daughter from a terrible dragon. Four oxcarts were needed to carry its body away from the castle.

I would like to see a dragon if Clotaire the Strong were there to rescue me. Then troubadours would write songs about us.

April 24th

Father still has not returned from Parthenay.

At the feast last night no one mentioned Saint George or the dragon. We have a new juggler, a dwarf who is as tall as my waist. He danced quite well for his size. His tiny shoes had bells sewn into the pointed toes. When he jumped onto the back of one of the hunting dogs, the dinner guests applauded while he rode the dog around the tables. There was much laughter and drinking of wine.

Marcabru was there with his lute. He walked the length of our table, singing about love and beautiful damsels, nodding toward me. I felt myself blush at his attentions. Marcabru's face is plain, but he dresses like a prince. His wool leggings had blue and white stripes, his tunic was green, and there was a peacock feather in his cap. While he stopped to tune the strings of his lute, he told me he has yet to finish the poem about Clotaire the Strong.

Later Petra and I stole to the roof for fresh air. It is peaceful to walk along the ramparts at night and look out over the dark countryside. The river Clain shimmered in the moonlight. We took off our headgear and untied our braids to let the wind loosen our hair. One of the watchmen walked toward us with a torch to see that we were all right. If Grandmère knew we were there without an escort, she would worry and scold. She says we must always take care to protect our virtue.

Another thought

Our troubadours often sing about King Arthur and his knights. One of their favorites is Sir Lancelot because of his valor on the battlefield and his gentleness with Queen Guinevere. The sad part about the story is that Lancelot fell in love with the beautiful queen, and she with him. This happened more than six hundred years ago, but people are still talking about their romance. I think of Lancelot every time I see Clotaire the Strong ride across the river in his suit of armor.

He and I are to meet tomorrow in the south garden. Madame arranged this. Last night when she came to tell me, she was wearing a jeweled belt my mother had given her the summer she died. Or at least that is the story Madame tells. Somehow she also inherited Mother's dresses, which she wears low to expose her full bosom. She is the prettiest of our ladies and likes to show off her dark hair and bare skin. Though she is busy about the palace listening for news, I trust her with some of my secrets.

My stomach hurts today, I think from eating too many honey cakes.

April 25th

Father is home again.

After handing the reins of his horse to his squire, he strode into the courtyard. He wore a red shirt under a long blue tunic that was adorned with silver buttons. Leather boots came to his knees. He is much taller than I am, and I could feel the strength in his arms when he embraced me.

"Is it true?" I asked him. "Are you friends with the pope again?"

"I think so," he answered. He explained that first there would be messengers between here and Rome, letters written, documents signed, and so forth. Pope Innocent may or may not pardon Father. If he does, it might still be months before Father is allowed to step inside a church again.

It is a situation Father could have avoided. It upsets me that so many people hate him.

"Are you through fighting with everyone?" I asked.

He touched the sword at his side. "It depends," he said. Then he looked down at me with a smile. Taking my chin in his palm, he said, "You are as lovely as your mother, *ma chèrie*. You are the talk of every man I meet."

I tilted my head away from him, irritated that he had changed the subject. "Please don't fight anymore, Father." I curtsied, then walked away.

Time for bed. Madame has just come in with a cup of hot wine to help me sleep.

Late, near midnight

With the wine, Madame brought bad news that has kept me awake. My candle has a few minutes left, so I will try to write it down while there is still light.

One of our vassals, Count William of Angoulême, plans to revolt! He is gathering others to side with him, including Baron William of Lezay. He is the castellan of our hunting lodge in Talmont, that is, keeper of the castle. I call him a cur because of the way he winks at me and because of his bad manners. At a banquet some months ago neither man bothered to stand when Father entered the great hall. They were too busy raising their cups for more wine. But oh, how they bowed and smiled when they saw me. I could tell they were enchanted by my presence, but I could also see how they hated my father by the way they exchanged glances and rolled their eyes when he spoke. As for the count of Angoulême, I call him the Spider. His hands were everywhere on the ladies-in-waiting and on the maids who served him. He even reached for me before I slapped his stubbly cheek.

It troubles me to think of those two plotting against us. Tomorrow I am going to tell Clotaire the Strong about them. I want him to personally see to my safety and Petronilla's.

Now my thoughts soften, remembering our time in the garden the other day. Clotaire and I sat near the fountain so that no one could eavesdrop through the sound of the splashing water, although our talk was not of a secret matter. It was the closest I have come to really looking at him, and how I enjoyed doing so! He told me he is eighteen years old and is an orphan, raised by one of my grandfather's knights. That is how he came into his fine suit of armor.

I like the way Clotaire wears his hair tied behind his neck with a leather string. His eyes are blue. Alas . . . my candle is out!

May 3rd

For days rain has been our companion, but this afternoon it was finally dry enough to go outside and sit in the sunshine. Petra and I studied in the courtyard with our tutor — more Latin verbs! To our delight we saw Father walking through the archway toward us. He was wearing his ducal breastplate; the polished silver shone bright over his black velvet sleeves. With a wave of his hand he dismissed our teacher then stood before us, smiling.

We set our books down, for we had not seen him cheerful in a long time. Ever since our mother and brother died six years ago, Father has been more moody than usual. His vassals call him a sour, ill-tempered beast, but he is not that way with us. As he stood there, he glanced up at the clouds, his face thoughtful.

After a moment he said, "*Mes filles*, I have some news. At long last you are to have a new mother and, in due time, a baby brother. I will wed the widow Emma of Cognac."

Petra looked at me with wide eyes. I did not know what to say.

May 6th

Everyone in the palace was whispering about Father's plans. Petra and I spent the day on our rock, far from the eyes and ears of the ladies and Grandmère. We are happy for him, that he will no longer be alone. But we suspect he wants to wed just so that he can have a son. We already have two brothers, but they are illegitimate and cannot inherit any of Father's land. Joscelin and Big William were born to women of uncertain character. We have met these half brothers several times, but are not allowed to socialize with them.

Emma will be duchess of Aquitaine. That would mean that a boy born to her and Father would inherit all of Aquitaine. If my real brother, Willie, were still alive, a marriage would not be so urgent.

I have heard stories of cruel stepmothers and worry that Emma will force us to live in an abbey, far away. We are used to being first in Father's heart. My spirit would be crushed if he let her do this.

Another matter troubling me is what I overheard in the library this morning. Some of Father's advisers were discussing Emma in grave tones. She is the daughter of the viscount of Limoges. Father has authority over all the lands in Limousin and Cognac, but the families there want him to stay away. They believe that with each visit he gets richer and they get poorer. They must pay him with chickens, hogs, vegetables, eggs, bags of flour, and barrels of wine. Over the years he has so angered these vassals that they may rise up against us if he insists on marrying Emma.

I love my papa, but I do not want a war on account of his wealth. He owns the largest duchy in all of France, even more land than the king! There are men who would do anything to steal his holdings, to weaken his power.

Evening

Petra is being scolded this minute by Grandmère. She was found wearing Mother's strands of pearls while out playing. Not only that, but my sister also wore a small crown of diamonds, which had been one of our father's wedding gifts to Mother.

I can hear Grandmère's voice from down the hallway. "Treasures are not be taken out into the garden," she is saying. I shake my head, knowing it is useless to scold Petronilla. She will soon forget the lecture and return to what she was doing in the first place.

May 25th

Every night a maid takes the chamber pot from a cupboard and sets it on the floor by my bed. She lights a short candle that will last just an hour. Finally, she fluffs my quilt and draws the curtains around my bed so that it will be warm when I sleep. I wait for her to leave before slipping out to the hallway. My door is as tall as three men and heavy to pull open; it is impossible to silence its creaking. Even so, I am able to retrieve my diary from Willie's helmet without anyone seeing me.

It is by this short candle that I now write.

In the mornings I break my fast with bread dipped in wine. Today, as it was raining, I decided to honor Saint Bede, the patron of scholars, by studying instead of sewing. I am reading the works of Cicero, and the *Last Days of Socrates* by Plato. The Latin is not easy, but I go slowly, one sentence at a time. Our tutor says this sharpens the mind. He said I am fortunate to be literate because most girls my age do not know how to read. Most <u>people</u> do not know how to read. We are one of the few families in Aquitaine to own books.

May 28th

Petra and I were at the stables this morning, after our ride along the river. One of the grooms was singing a song, a passionate tune about love. He had heard it from the miller, who heard it from the blacksmith. The blacksmith heard it while sharpening the sword of Clotaire the Strong. And Clotaire had heard it from Father, who sang it while he strolled through the garden. It was about sweet Emma, his bride-to-be. I think Marcabru wrote it for him. Now everyone is singing Father's song. It is nearly as lusty as some of my grandfather's poems. I feel embarrassed, thinking of Father and Emma together.

The wedding is in two weeks. When I meet Emma, I will curtsy and try to be kind to her. Maybe she won't send us away if she sees what good daughters we are. I hope my sister doesn't say something silly.

The cooks are planning the wedding feast. It will be huge. Many cattle must be slaughtered to feed everyone, and untold numbers of ducks and peacocks. When I visited the baker this morning for some honeycomb, he threw his hands in the air while describing the cake he must bake. Father wants it to be the exact shape of our palace with miniature knights on top and tiny animals in the courtyard. It will take days to shape the pastries and color them with dyes. Then there must be dozens of smaller cakes with pretty scenes on top, such as forests and swans swimming on a lake.

I must end this for now. A seamstress is unfolding lengths of linen for my dress. It will take hours of me standing perfectly still for her to mark the cloth and pin up the folds. Then she'll take it apart and set to sewing. Petra is next.

Later, a quick note

Madame woke me before sunrise with horrifying news. Emma has been kidnapped! Father is beside himself with rage. I am on my way downstairs. I must find him before he does something he will later regret.

March 31st

At sunrise we all attended Mass — Grandmère, our ladies, Petra, and I — and took the Eucharist. Prayers were said to Saint Radegund for Emma's safe return. Radegund is the patron of Poitiers. The convent she started six hundred years ago is at the bottom of this hill, past the gate of the city, through the trees. I often visit her tomb, to light candles and think. I have been praying about other things in my heart, not for Emma. God forgive me . . . I do not want her to marry my father.

This morning when he tried to enter the church with us, the priest gently stopped him.

"I am sorry, Monsieur le Duc," he said. "Not until the pope gives word can you worship with us."

Before the sun was an hour high, Father rode out with some of his men. We could hear the galloping of horses across the bridge. Madame says he is searching for Emma.

June 1st

This afternoon Petra and I sat in the sunshine to do our counting lesson. We work with seedpods that are strung along a stick. They sound like tiny rattles as we push them back and forth to calculate numbers. We had just returned them to our tutor and were ready to study astronomy when Father appeared. He clapped his hands together and said we must pack immediately.

"Ducal progress," he said. He did not need to explain. This is something we do several times a year: travel through Aquitaine so that our father the duke can check on his lands and vassals. He has them kneel and renew their vows of loyalty to him. This is also when he collects the shares of food and livestock due him as their overlord.

But I wanted to know about Emma's kidnapping. When I asked, his face turned red. "It was that swine, Angoulême," he burst out. "I could kill him!"

"Can't you rescue her, Father?"

"It's too late," he cried.

It seems that the Spider, the count of Angoulême, stole into Emma's bedchamber and carried her outside to a waiting coach. Before the night was over, he had driven to an abbey where a priest married them. Emma had no say in the matter. Now she is just a lowly countess with a husband who can't keep his hands off the serving maids.

I am sorry for Father but said nothing, for fear my words would betray my happiness. Grandmère told me to write the longings of my heart in this diary. . . . Well, here is the truth: I am overjoyed. I did not want a new brother to take Willie's place. And I did not want a stepmother who might hate me.

June 2nd

The priest prayed this morning for all of Father's sailors who trade along our Aquitaine coast. But my prayers were for the rain to stop! Our trip to the seaside will take many long days. In the rain it will be most miserably muddy and cold.

Our chapel has even more pigeons up in the rafters, for it is a nice dry place. I am a bit nervous praying here because the stone floor is splattered with their droppings. One of our ladies had an unfortunate mess land on her shoulder.

Tomorrow we leave. We will spend the summer at Father's favorite hunting lodge, Talmont-by-the-Sea. I think it is his way of putting distance between him and the Spider. He usually seeks revenge over the slightest insult, so I'm puzzled why he is so quiet about losing Emma. Could it be that his experience with Father Bernard truly changed his heart?

June 3rd

A maid awoke Petra and me before sunup. We looked out the window and saw puddles along the paths, which meant it had rained all night. It is still drizzling as I write this. Porters are carrying down our trunks and baskets to load onto carts. This diary will fit inside the silk pouch Grandmère sewed for me, along with my quill and a flask of ink. The strap lies across my chest so that I can keep it close to me, under my cloak.

Petra says she wants her own diary because she has a secret. She will not tell me! It must have something to do with romance because she blushes when I ask her. But she is only twelve. . . . What could it possibly be?

Niort, halfway between Poitiers and the ocean

This old castle is cozy as long as we stand by the fire. As in our palace in Poitiers, the rooms are cold and damp. Petra and I were soaked to the skin when we walked up the long steps into the great hall. Our dresses and hair dripped all the way to our chamber, where maids helped us into dry clothes. That is where we are now, in an upstairs room overlooking the river. There are still dozens of wagons coming this way along the road. On a ducal progress everyone comes: the bakers and blacksmiths, ladies and maids, knights and squires, the animal keeper with cages for Father's and my falcons. Even cows and goats come.

Were it not for the rain, we would be able to hear the wagons rattling with cooking pots and the noise of chickens.

The reason we were so wet is our coach broke a wheel one league away. Though there was room for us on a baggage cart, we were weary from so many hours of sitting and bumping along the rutted road. Petra and I decided the rain wouldn't bother us if we walked the rest of the way. To save our shoes we carried them; the mud was sticky and cold between our toes. Servants tried to keep us from leaving, but we outran their voices. From the hill we could see down to the fortress with its moat. Some of Father's chevaliers, his knights, were already there, leading their horses to stables.

Grandmère didn't miss us because she was busy in another coach, where one of her ladies was about to have a baby.

Evening

Petra and I are sharing a bed tonight because we are still chilled from our run through the rain. After the maids had drawn the curtains about us, we overheard them discussing the duke, our father. It seems he has offended the servants here. He was furious because there were no geese prepared for his dinner. We could hear his shouts echo through the cold hallways.

I feel sorry for the maids and cooks. No one knew we were coming until our knights announced themselves at the drawbridge. Niort is one of Father's many castles. It is his right to come and go as he pleases, as do the pigeons in our chapel. But doing so often upsets those who live here when we are away. They never know when he will show up.

I will blow out this candle with a heavy heart. I wish for once that whispers we heard about Father were pleasant. I wish he would take the advice of Father Bernard and stop thundering curses upon the people who serve him.

June 6th

We are traveling again, heading west toward the coast. At long last it is warm. The sun is out and drying the muddy road. We have stopped near an orchard to rest our horses. The plums and peaches are not yet ripe, so we didn't pick the trees. I can see the abbey where Grandmère is taking her ladies to pray. They are walking along a shaded path, their long, flowing sleeves nearly touching the ground.

The forest is beyond. Each year Father gives the monks permission to cut trees for firewood.

June 12th, traveling

The ocean is near! There is a wonderful smell of salt air and fish. Petra and I want to run ahead of the wagons and be first to step into the sea. But we are being closely watched. Grandmère scolded us for hurrying ahead to Niort. For some time she could not find us and worried we had been kidnapped like Emma. She said we deserve punishment, but she does not have the heart to whip us. Then she reminded us that girls who misbehave are often sent away to convents. It is up to the nuns to whip or not. I do not want this to happen! A nunnery would be torture even though I love God and love reading Scripture.

Sometimes I want to scream from sitting still.

Yesterday Clotaire rode alongside my coach. It is too hard to speak to each other above the noise of wheels and harnesses, but we managed a few shouted words. When I pointed to his horse, he grabbed my hand and leaned down to kiss my fingers. I felt myself flush with pleasure.

I do not care if Grandmère saw.

Afternoon

The baby born to Grandmère's lady died this morning. The poor little thing is covered up and wrapped in linen, as small as a loaf of bread. There is no priest to pray over it, so we will bury it ourselves. If we wait until we find the next church, the body will take on a foul odor. A squire is digging a hole by a lilac bush.

June 13th
Talmont-by-the-Sea

Last week I thought Poitiers was my favorite place on earth, but now I remember how much I love the ocean. The village of Talmont sits high on a headland where the wind keeps the air cool even on hot days. Far below, waves break against the rocks. The church is so close to the edge of the cliff, part of its wall crumbled into the sea. This was a few years ago. A little boy who was sitting there swinging his legs fell to his death. I did not see it happen, but the memory of that tragic moment makes my throat tight. That little boy was my brother, Willie. This was the first of two tragedies that summer.

I will write later about the other.

An hour ago Petronilla came into our room after walking along the shore with the ladies. Her cheeks were red from the sun and wind. She set a basket on the table, full of tiny yellow flowers picked from the sand dunes. They were for me! As she was weaving them into a wreath for my hair she burst into tears. I asked what was troubling her.

"I wanted there to be a wedding," she cried. "Now we'll never see all those pretty cakes."

When I told her that no wedding meant there would be no stepmother to send us away, her face brightened. She became so cheerful that she blurted out her secret: Marcabru has written a song about her! It is called "Petronilla, the Sweetest Flower of All." He is going to sing it tomorrow at the banquet.

I assured my sister her secret was safe with me, though I have written it here. Now I must find a new hiding place for my diary. There is an underground passage that leads from the castle to the sea, but it is often muddy from the tides.

June 14th

Petronilla and I were wandering around the lower floors, where the laundry women work. Near the wine cellar is a suite of rooms for the baron of Lezay. As castellan he is in charge when Father isn't here. He also acts as a warden for settling small disputes among the serfs. When we turned down the corridor we could see into his office, for the door was ajar. A torch lit the room, where he was sitting at a small table. A maid was pouring wine into a goblet and another maid was sitting on his lap! The sight of him made me hurry my sister away, upstairs to the sunlight.

I do not know why Father would allow such a man in our castle.

June 24th

It took two full days before the baggage train was unpacked. Once again there are familiar voices of courtiers and servants busy in the halls. Our palace is near a stream, not far from the village. Beyond the outer wall the blacksmiths have set up their sheds and hot fires. Throughout the day I can hear their hammers clink against iron. There is always work to be done: sharpening knives and swords, forging new helmets, repairing armor and chain mail. It takes them hours upon hours to shape the tiny iron chains then solder them together. Willie's small shirt and leggings took days to craft.

I am writing this in my apartment, where a narrow window looks out along the rugged coastline. The opening has a casement with squares of glass so that I can close it when there are storms, but today the sea breeze is pleasant. In the garden below, minstrels are practicing for this evening's entertainment. I can hear Marcabru's voice. I wonder if he has finished his poem about Clotaire the Strong.

Oh, a chevalier has galloped into the courtyard bearing news. I will close these pages for now.

Evening

Such excitement . . . The horseman announced travelers: Count Geoffrey of Anjou arrived an hour later with some of his chevaliers. Petra and I peered from the stairs down to the great hall and saw the visitors. I decided we must put on our loveliest dresses right away. The count is taller and even more striking than Father. Geoffrey the Handsome is our name for him.

When he pushed back his hood of chain mail, his hair fell to his shoulders in brown curls. The tunic over his armor was blue with a golden crest. He and Father greeted each other warmly. I liked the look of his face and muscular arms. He could easily slay a dragon then carry me to safety. I am sure of it.

The reason for Count Geoffrey's visit? He has invited Father to go to war. He is just twenty-three years old and needs help invading Normandy.

And without thinking twice, Father said yes! I worry he has made another terrible decision. It seems he is trying to make up for having done nothing about Emma's kidnapping.

June 29th

Every morning bells ring to announce Mass. Today I visited the church that overlooks the sea. A breeze followed me into the cool, dark chapel until the heavy door closed. The priest prayed to Saint Peter for the fishermen who go out in little boats.

I think my prayers are selfish, for I want to go with Father. I want to ride alongside Geoffrey the Handsome. Even though women are forbidden to go to war, Father could let me — he is duke of Aquitaine! The blacksmith could make me a suit of chain mail like Willie's and I could carry a knife. The other day I tried to lift Father's sword, but it was too heavy, even holding it with both hands. Its sharp steel blade stabbed the dirt when I dropped it. My arms were shaking from the effort.

June 30th

Our castellan, Baron Lezay, is too friendly with me. He surprised me in the herb garden when I was bending down to pick some rosemary. I felt him brush against my hip as he passed on the stepping-stones. For a moment I thought it was an accident, but when I looked up and saw his grin, I knew he had done it on purpose.

"How dare you!" I said. "Some day you shall regret being so bold, sir." Then I slapped him with the back of my hand, drawing blood where my ring scraped him.

I'm still angry as I write this. I've warned Petronilla to stay as far away from him as possible. Since he lives in this castle throughout the year, he acts as if he owns it. I wish Father would replace him. But Lezay is one of the few vassals who does not melt under Father's explosive temper. He is allowed to stay because no one else will.

This evening I told Father what had happened in the garden. He was so distracted by the excitement of going to war, he didn't understand what I meant.

"It's your beauty, Eleanor," he said, leaning over to kiss me on each cheek. "Men find you irresistible."

July 1st

Our midday meals last at least two hours. It is dull to sit when we could be out in the sunshine. The only part that is entertaining is when Petra and I are getting dressed. We paint each other's cheeks, then try on Mother's earrings. I wish I could remember what she looked like!

Today when we made our entrance, there were two rows of knights waiting for us. As we walked between them toward Father's table, I could feel their admiring eyes upon us. The company bowed at the waist, each man sweeping a hand to the floor.

Clotaire the Strong smiled at me as my skirt brushed over his feet. "M'lady," he said. At the sound of his voice I felt my face grow warm. I enjoy his attentions and wish to return them, even if he is just a village orphan.

At dinner Marcabru again sang about King Arthur. When he told the story of Lancelot's love for Queen Guinevere, he looked right at me, then at Clotaire. For some reason this made me feel so nervous that I did not touch my plate of honey cakes.

July 2nd

Petra and I were escorted on a walk this morning by six knights and five of Grandmère's ladies (she has twelve). There are robbers who hide in the trees along this road, so my sister and I must have protection. How I yearn to be alone! I miss our secret rock in Poitiers where we could talk without people watching us and listening.

Behind us the falconer drove a cart carrying a falcon cage, for I wanted to fly my bird. With us also were minstrels, maids, and a cook. The heat made my dress feel heavy, so Petra and I waded in a stream to cool off. We splashed the cold water on our faces and necks, but when Grandmère saw what we were doing, she clapped her hands for us to get out immediately. "It is not proper for ladies to show themselves," she said, but how I wanted to disobey her! It was so hot that I felt miserable.

I wondered about everyone else. The ladies wore layers of skirts under their dresses and kirtles, sleeves covering their wrists, and wimples over their heads. And the chevaliers — one fainted in the sun! Their heavy armor must be unbearable. Where their helmets touch their cheeks, some have raw blisters.

At noon we stopped at the water mill to eat a light dinner: sardines, boiled eggs, bread, and onions. In a nearby orchard we picked apricots. The trees were short enough that we did not need ladders. Petra and I lay in the grass to watch the clouds. We enjoyed listening to the splashing of the mill's huge wheel. As it turns, it creaks, and there is a thumping sound from its wooden cogs. To me, this sound is more soothing than a minstrel's harp.

When I noticed Grandmère had fallen asleep in the shade, I nudged Petra and we quietly hurried to the river-bank. Upstream was a mound of twigs from a beaver's hut. It had formed a dam with a waterfall flowing around it down to a pool below. A perfect place to swim. I glanced over my shoulder at our knights. They were guarding us from a discreet distance.

Petra and I stepped behind a bush, then, as quickly as we could, unlaced our dresses and stepped out of them. Wearing only our shifts, we jumped into the water as we used to do when we were younger. I swam under-water with my eyes open and could see my sister's bare legs kicking, and she could see mine. Oh, it was the most pleasing interlude we have had in a long time!

To continue

When Grandmère woke from her nap, she said nothing about our wet hair. Sometimes I think she pretends not to notice things because she's tired of scolding us.

The falconer gave me a long leather glove to protect me from the bird's sharp talons. Then he opened the cage. She is a white gyrfalcon, larger and fiercer than most of the browns. Her name is Snow-Jer. When she perches on my arm, she is so heavy that I can stand it for only a moment. I remove her little leather hood so she'll be able to see. With hardly an effort, she lifts her wings to fly. The weight of her taking off pushes my arm down to my side.

What a beautiful bird and a good hunter. She always returns with a partridge or rabbit. The straps on her legs have tiny bells attached so that we can hear when she lands on her prey. I whistle through my teeth, and soon we spot her rising in the air, coming our way.

More later. A page just walked in with a message from Father.

Before supper

Father was waiting for me on the cliff, overlooking the rough blue sea. He smiled at me as he spoke, but the wind carried away his voice. He had to shout so that I could hear. It is too dangerous for a girl to go on an invasion, he told me. Normandy is far north from here. Petronilla and I must stay in Talmont, where there is safety behind our stone walls. Also, the summer heat will be more bearable for us if we are by the ocean.

I curtsied to show my respect, but inside I felt tight with worry. I do not want him to go away. If he is wounded, who will care for him? And if he is killed . . . I do not know what Petra and I would do without our father. The cur Lezay will try to take over this castle, and who knows what he'll do to us?

The sunroom in which I now sit looks out onto one of the courtyards. I can hear the clinking of the blacksmiths' hammers. There is much to be done before Father can join Geoffrey the Handsome. His knights must have their swords sharpened and shields tested for strength. Even horses will have masks to protect their long faces. Father seems delighted to be busy again. When Emma was kidnapped he was furious, but he could not get her back without making war. Maybe going to someone else's battle is a way to keep peace in Aquitaine.

July 6th

I awoke before dawn to the sound of hoofbeats. I stepped out of bed and hurried across the room to look out the window. There were torchlights moving in a line away from our fortress. Father was leaving! I had known this day would soon be here, but still I felt a lump in my throat. When we said our good-byes at the banquet last night, we were all in happy spirits.

Marcabru had surprised us with new songs. The one about Petronilla was so cheerful that everyone in the great hall laughed. Then he turned toward me. The delicate music from his lute brought tears to my eyes. His words formed a romantic poem about Clotaire the Strong . . . how he has eyes for only me, Eleanor, daughter of Aquitaine.

As the hours wore on, Father's dwarf and acrobats helped me forget this was a farewell evening. Not until this morning did I remember. Church bells rang for Mass, but I stayed in my chamber.

Later, some upsetting news

When I was in the library reading, Madame came in and stood by the window. Looking out she said, "There is trouble, m'lady. Now that your father is gone, there is a plot concerning you and Petronilla."

I sat up straight. "I'm listening."

"Some barons are planning to take you as wives," she said.

I studied Madame's face. Her eyes were outlined with charcoal, her cheeks painted pink. The bracelets on her arm clinked as she pointed outside. I believe she was telling the truth, for she has yet to report news that isn't so.

When I asked which barons were plotting, one of the names did not surprise me. Lezay. It was as I suspected. Because he is Talmont's castellan, he thinks he should be able to take what he wants.

"*Merci*, Madame." I dismissed her with instructions to alert Clotaire the Strong. Petra and I must be more cautious when we go out. Perhaps we should listen more carefully to Grandmère.

July 13th

A summer rain has us indoors. Petra is with the ladies, practicing proper walking ("head high!") and sitting ("hands in lap, knees together!"). I excused myself to use the privy and have not returned. Oh, joy . . . to be alone. The alcove here is in a quiet hall, where there are shelves of books reaching up to the ceiling. For light it has a double window that bows out over a garden. It is here where I felt something wobble under the cushion: a loose stone the size of my hand. I lifted it to find it hollow underneath, a perfect place in which to hide this diary.

Now with some moments to myself, I can write about those close to my heart. First, Grandmère.

For nearly fourteen years I have been under her care, even when Mother was alive. She is not beautiful, but I adore her. She has the grace and good manners of a queen. When her ladies brush her long hair, it falls to her ankles. The color at the ends is blond, like a hem of gold. Then up to her shoulders it changes to reddish brown. The crown of her head is white. She says her hair reveals the three stages of her life: childhood, a young woman, and now a grandmother. After fleas and nits have been combed out, her ladies plait it, then twist it onto the nape of her neck.

Over this she wears a wimple that fastens under her chin with a silver brooch.

Noble families send their daughters to learn from my grandmother. This is the first year we haven't had eight or ten other girls living under our roof. Most of them married last June, when it was warm enough to take a bridal bath. Some now live in Paris, in the royal household of King Louis the Fat, and are ladies for the queen. That is how well Grandmère trained them.

Someday I, too, will marry. The husband Father chooses for me will not be a peasant or a goldsmith or a squire. He will be highborn, possibly a chevalier or even a prince. Only one man in all of France ranks above my Father: the king himself. Our family's position means that my sister and I could marry royalty. Grandmère says that is why I must become refined and educated.

Oh, the rain has stopped and Petra is here. She wants us to explore the pools below the cliffs while the tide is low.

Before bed

Candles have been lit in the fireplace of my room. The light reflects well against the golden stones and gives off some warmth. The night breeze coming in the window is cool. I can hear waves breaking in the distance.

Back to Grandmère. She has never whipped me, though the cooks and laundry women and baker tell her she should. I am too headstrong, they say — I should spend more time on ladies' arts, such as needlework and spinning wool. Alas, they do not understand my heart, how it is torture for me to do those things hour after hour.

I forgot to say that Grandmère traveled to Paris a few years ago, to meet the king. The reason he is called Louis the Fat is because of his immense size. He can no longer boost himself up into his saddle to ride his horse. And a new royal carriage was built, one that would not collapse under his weight. Grandmère said the king was kind to her, but he smelled like a mule. When she rose from her curtsy, she noticed that the hem of his robe was adorned with rubies. His swollen feet were in slippers encrusted with emeralds.

She said Father is thinking about matching me with the king's son! He is fourteen and ready to be married. For days now I've wondered what it would be like to be a princess in Paris. It is quite a journey north, where it is colder and people are not as fond of merrymaking as we are in sunny Aquitaine. And what if the boy is fat like his father? I do not want to marry a giant who won't enjoy parties.

July 25th

At Mass this morning the chapel was full of villagers. Petra and I sat in an alcove reserved for our family. Everyone else stood, listening to the monastic choir. The monks wear dark, hooded robes and sing of God's goodness with deep, beautiful voices. Because of their slow rhythm I was able to understand their Latin.

In the back of the church by the tall wooden doors there are stone columns. It smells of urine and worse. I have seen men relieve themselves here and women squat within the privacy of their dresses. Petra and I think this is vulgar.

Many of Father's castles have enclosed privies that jut out over a moat. It is the most pleasant way for waste to be washed away. I know of monks who have built their abbeys like this, with the latrines emptying over a river. These tiny privy rooms are also called garderobes. During warmer months our cloaks are hung up in here, from pegs hammered between the stones. Grandmère says the stink keeps away moths that eat fur and wool. Thus our robes are "guarded." I would prefer my clothes to be stored in cedar chests, but alas, it is easier to travel without all that luggage.

Back to the Mass: Prayers were to Saint James the Greater. He was a fisherman who walked with Jesus and witnessed his miracles. Pilgrims journey to Spain, where James is buried. They say that just by touching his tomb, it is possible for lepers to be healed and the blind to see.

July 29th

I love summer by the sea. Before vespers, our evening prayers, Petra and I explored the tide pools. We found an octopus whose head was the size of a plum. We've been gathering shells and starfish and have made a garden full of these and other dead sea creatures. Grandmère holds her nose at the odor, but it doesn't bother us.

Twenty-three days since Father left. Messengers have brought word that the invasion is in progress. He has not been wounded, but his horse was killed by an enemy sword. The priest says there are many saints we can pray to for Father's safe return, but I don't know if they truly hear me.

Later

Madame passed a note to me during dinner:

> *Baron William Lezay was seen with Viscount Barber and a band of ruffians who live in the woods.*

I wish Father would hurry home.

August 2nd

Today one of the baker's sons, a boy of about five years, complained that he felt so ill he feared he would pass out. I hurried him away from the ovens, through a gate to the courtyard. No sooner were we outside than he vomited a white curly mass. It looked like a pile of linen strips. But when it started moving and crawling, I realized it was worms. Horrid, long things. I stopped myself from shrieking because I did not want to frighten him. The poor boy began to wail, anyway. One of our physicians gave him a draught of mint and charcoal mixed with wormwood, of course.

An hour later I was picking flowers with a village girl. She was pretty, with a wreath of posies in her hair and feet brown from the sun. I had noticed something white in the corner of her eye that seemed to be moving. When I looked closer and realized it was a maw worm working its way out of the girl's head, I cried out for the physician. In moments he was there, holding the worm in his palm until the entire thing slithered out. It was nearly the length of my arm, a dreadful sight. He said these are the worst kind because they eat away your insides.

I have felt sick all day from watching this. Now every time my eye itches, or my nose or ear, I will worry a maw worm is in me, trying to get out.

Later, a terrible event

I am so upset from this afternoon's events that I must quickly write them down before I forget anything.

This is what happened. When the sun was overhead, Petra and I mounted our horses and were escorted through the main gate, across the bridge, out to the road. We were to spend the afternoon along the river. The knights were dressed in full armor, their horses in brightly colored skirts. Flags announced we were the daughters of Aquitaine. It felt as if we were on our way to a jousting tournament, such was our finery. The jangling of harnesses and pounding hooves was so loud that I almost did not hear Petra scream.

Before my very eyes, a rough-looking man astride a stallion galloped into our midst and took hold of my sister around her waist. It happened so quickly, I cannot blame our men for being surprised. Their helmets block their sight, I am sure of it. They did not see him coming from the woods.

Instantly, Clotaire reached over and pulled me into his own saddle, though my dress was so bulky it felt that I would slip off. He spurred his horse and headed back for Talmont, followed by six other escorts. I screamed my sister's name and twisted around to catch sight of her. The hoofbeats clopping atop the wooden bridge drowned out my voice. When I was safe inside the walls, Clotaire hurried me up to the roof, where we could see out toward the forest. The sun gleaming on the armor of two dozen knights reflected like a giant mirror. I caught a glimpse of Petra's dress. She was upon the horse of another knight, riding fast toward the palace. I recognized him as one of our younger men because of the red tunic he wore over his chain mail. My sister had been rescued.

I was filled with relief, and only then did I start to tremble. My knees felt weak. Bracing myself against the wall, I leaned out over the stone ledge so that I could see better. Some of the chevaliers had dismounted and were holding the kidnapper. His arms were tied behind his back, and he was being dragged down to the dirt. When I saw the glint of sunlight on a raised sword, I turned away.

Did Lezay plan this?

August 3rd

My sister and I are still distressed from yesterday. Our knights rounded up a group of men who live in the forest. Six of them were beheaded; the others fled. Though it is unlikely another bandit will try to steal us for wives, Grandmère has forbidden us to leave the fortress. I will listen to her this time. Madame told us that her husband and others searched but could not find any trace of Viscount Barber or Lezay. We may never know if they were involved.

Night, a full moon

I am too nervous to sleep.

This morning there was a sweet scent of roses on the breeze. I felt sad until I remembered why. It was on just such a day that Mother and I last spoke. We were walking along the shore, where shallow waves soaked the hems of our dresses. We carried our shoes. I was eight years old and did not mind that her ladies and several knights followed us.

Suddenly, she clutched her side, then collapsed in the wet sand. The knights carried her immediately up the steep hill to the village. A fever made her delirious. How I cried for her to wake up and say my name. By the following sunset she was gone. My only comfort in her death came some weeks later, when Willie was killed: She did not have to suffer over losing him, and they are together in heaven. I read this for myself in Saint Paul's epistle to the Corinthians: "To be absent from the body is to be present with the Lord."

It is late. Moonlight is coming in through the window. I dismissed the maids after they turned down my bed and lit this little candle. It is down to its last flicker. As soon as it goes out, I will hurry to the alcove and hide my diary beneath the cushion. Then maybe sleep will find me.

Another thought

The days are hotter. We are plagued by flies that swarm around the latrines and garbage pits. They drift in through our windows, along with foul odors, and do not leave us. These are the only things about summer I do not enjoy: flies and stink.

August 6th

Petra and I spent the afternoon on the beach, surrounded by knights with ready swords. We were wading among the tide pools when we heard a cry. We looked up. Standing at the edge of the cliff was a squire waving for us to come. Not until we had climbed the path did we hear him.

"Monsieur le Duc, your father, is returning!" he said.

In the distance we could see the road from the north. Dust rose above small dots that were horses.

It was an hour before they approached the other side of the river, close enough to where we could see their colored pennants and their helmets gleaming in the sunlight. Petra and I ran to the outer gate where Father would enter. We couldn't wait to see him.

But the father who slid off his horse in the courtyard was not the same man we'd seen on our last evening together. His cheeks were sunken; the beard he'd grown over the past weeks was matted with mud. He held out his arms to us, but said nothing. Only a heavy sigh escaped his lips.

Later

I am writing before bed. The banquet this evening was lively with all of Father's acrobats and jesters and dancers with tambourines. Marcabru was there in his blue-striped leggings to sing for us. Servers brought platters of duck and venison; maids carried about bowls of water so that we could wash the grease from our fingers. One of the dogs caught a rat under the table. I wish I could say these things cheered Father, but they did not. Each time I smiled at him, he turned away. <u>Is he somehow disappointed with me?</u> I worried. <u>Does he blame me for my sister being nearly kidnapped?</u>

Petra and I asked him about the Normandy invasion, if it succeeded or not, but he just looked down at his hands. His knights were toasting one another as if there had been victory, but Father was not telling us what had happened. He seems haunted by something.

Since he is not allowed into church, tomorrow I am going to ask the priest to come here.

August 7th

I have acted dishonorably. This morning I hid myself behind one of the large tapestries hanging against a wall in Father's chamber so that I could hear what he and the priest talked about. Eavesdropping is a sin, I know. . . .

To my selfish relief, Father's mood is not because of anything I've done, but is from remorse. He is filled with shame for cruelties he committed on the battlefield. Our friend, Count Geoffrey the Handsome, received such a bloody wound to the foot that he returned to his castle in Anjou, unable to walk. The invasion was a disaster, Father confessed. He never again wants to hurt another human being.

When I heard sobbing, I thought perhaps it was the priest. The tapestry hiding me was woven with wool and had a small moth hole at eye level. Through this I was able to see that the man weeping was my proud father, the duke of Aquitaine. I could not believe it. He was on his knees, repenting for his sins.

August 13th

There are more hours of daylight than darkness. How I love summer. The air is pleasant because of wind coming off the sea. I visited Father in the garden, where he was picking melons. I had never seen him do servants' work before. He was wearing the loose white shirt of a peasant and coarse trousers. No ducal vest or jewels on his fingers.

He said he had two surprises for me. When he told me the first one I had to sit down in the shade of a tree to keep from fainting. It is this:

He is so desperately sorry about taking part in the Normandy war, he is going on a pilgrimage! To Santiago de Compostela, to the tomb of Saint James the Greater. Father wants to be healed of his grieving heart and commit his life to serving God. I was stunned by his next surprise. He is putting his affairs in order so that upon his death I will become duchess. And it is urgent that he find a husband for me.

When he said this, I wanted to crumble inside. "Papa, why must I marry so soon . . . are you planning to die?" I cried.

"No, *ma fille*," he said, "not planning to. But pilgrimages are long, dangerous journeys. Many who go do not return alive."

Because Father has no male heir to succeed him, I will inherit the duchy of Aquitaine. Oh, how my heart pounded at his words. My courage failed me. I did not ask if he would hunt for the men who plotted to kidnap us. Or who he thinks should be my husband.

Even now, as I write this by the side of my bed, I am trembling.

Later

Father is planning a celebration for my fourteenth birthday, which falls during summer; no one remembers the date I was born. He is inviting his most loyal vassals to come and swear fealty to me. This means they promise to protect and defend me from this moment forward. He thinks I will be safer.

Before bed

When we return to Poitiers, I will take Petra to Saint Radegund's tomb. We are fond of her story:

Even though she was queen of the northern French kingdom of Merovingia, her cruel husband would beat her. To save herself, she ran south with two of her maids, but he chased her. The only place she could hide was in a newly planted cornfield. She and her ladies threw themselves down into the dirt. By God's mercy, the corn stalks immediately grew several feet tall. Just minutes later her husband and his men galloped by on their horses, cursing because they were unable to find the queen. Radegund was so thankful for this miracle that she dedicated her life to God, became a nun, and started a convent in Poitiers.

I think of Queen Radegund's bravery and believe that I, too, am brave. I want to walk with Father to Santiago de Compostela. Maybe by touching the tomb of Saint James, I will be cured of my selfishness.

Also, going on a pilgrimage would mean I could delay marriage.

August 27th

Two weeks have passed since I've written. My birthday celebration was grand!

After Father sent word throughout Aquitaine about the fealty ceremony for me, his knights and squires began arriving on horseback. The countryside around our palace by the sea began to resemble a pageant. Tents were pitched along the streams with colorful flags and pennants. Horses were corralled inside brush fences.

Some knights brought along their wives to cook for them. Many chevaliers are from noble families, but some are just villagers who are loyal to my father. For many, the suit of chain mail is too expensive, so their armor is made from leather. Their shields are cut from stiff cowhide. I have seen jousting tournaments in which villagers such as these ride against each other. They practice fighting, but I think are no match for a man in iron. I cringe to think what would happen to them on a battlefield.

Later

When the ceremony began, I had been in my gown for three hours already. The heat was sweltering that afternoon, and the fabric of my undersmock itched wretchedly against my skin. At my request Petronilla stood by my side because she brings me great comfort. I can push my foot against hers, under our skirts, and she immediately knows my thoughts. We do this often. But there is always a danger we might burst into laughter at the wrong moment.

This unfortunately did happen when we were in the great hall.

It was after Father's speech and the bowing of the knights as they stood before us. The room was quiet while they said oaths of loyalty to me, their Lady Eleanor, Daughter of Aquitaine, Poitou, and Gascony. I watched their faces — old and young, some handsome, some with terrible scars — and felt moved by their tender words. These good men were swearing to protect and defend me, even at the cost of their own lives. Would I ever be able to show my gratitude? I took a deep breath to hold back my tears. Just then Petra's foot nudged mine.

With a nod of her head she directed my eyes to the far end of the hall. Three of our hunting dogs were under a table, digging through the rushes that cover the floor. This straw is usually filled with bones and bread crusts from previous meals. But this time they had uncovered a serving boy and a maid who had sneaked away from their duties to steal a kiss. The sight of them scrambling from their hiding place with the dogs happily wagging their tails struck me as comical. I clapped my hand over my mouth, but still my laugh was heard. All eyes turned to me. Petra made a sound like a hiccup.

A stern look from Grandmère silenced us.

When the ceremony ended, Father signaled the musicians to play. A jester jumped onto a table to juggle oranges. Servants appeared from the outdoor kitchen holding platters high. The banquet lasted long into the night, with most of our guests drinking too much wine and many falling asleep in the rushes. There they stayed until morning. I am thankful for a bed away from the noise and one that does not stink of rotten food and vomit.

September 1st
On the road

Our summer by the sea has ended. We are traveling once again, on our way back to Poitiers. Because Father wants to complete his ducal progress before his pilgrimage, we are taking the long way home, south, along the Charente River to Cognac. This is where our finest vineyards are. And Emma, who was to be our stepmother, lived here before her first husband died.

The heat is fierce as we ride inland, away from the coast. We are staying at one of our vassals' estates for a night. The family was pleased to host us, but I heard whispering among their servants. No one believes Father's new passion. They think he just wants to go to Spain for more soldiers, so he'll have more power. Word has reached us that his vassals in Limousin are so distrustful they are stirring up a rebellion. Lezay is among them, and the count of Angoulême. Is it not enough that he stole Father's bride? Must this Spider wage war, too?

No matter what others think, I know the truth! A wonderful change has come over Father. He calls himself a "new man in Christ, a new creation." Indeed, our maids and courtiers have noticed he no longer erupts in temper, but is patient with them. He has been giving away his fine clothes to the villagers. The jeweled rings he used to wear are no longer on his hands. He does not know I saw this, but he gave a ruby pendant to one of our cooks and some gold chains to the laundry women. What they will do with their new wealth, I do not know. Maybe they will buy a pig or a cow, for they cannot own land unless Father grants that to them as well.

Afternoon

We have stopped the caravan for our noon meal. I am writing while sitting by a stream. Petra is napping beside me in the shade. A few days from now we will reach our castle.

This morning when the grass was still damp with dew, I walked to a small church with Father. Even though he is still excommunicated, he went inside. He prayed on his knees, speaking out loud like a man who personally knows God. I peeked at him over my folded hands and felt tears in my throat. I do not want him to leave.

September 3rd
Cognac

We have settled nicely in Cognac. The river Charente flows outside the city wall, bringing a cool breeze that makes the heat bearable. Petra and I spent the morning in one of our courtyards, under the shade of a grape arbor. We could see through a gate to the riverbank, where boys floated little boats they made from sticks. Fishermen come in the late afternoons. When I am here in Cognac, I think <u>this</u> is my favorite place. I can tell the harvest will be soon, for the air smells sweet from grapes.

September 15th

It is early; Petra still sleeps. Maids are arranging our dresses, for today we are going into the countryside to hawk. Because the knights have sworn fealty to me, I may say which ones accompany us. I chose five plus Clotaire the Strong. My feelings for him grow each time we're together. But in my heart I feel sad: He is not on Father's list of suitable husbands.

Late, all is quiet

Such a day! I will try to put it all down before this candle goes, then hide my diary. Alas, the only place I've found for it is inside my pillow.

Petra has her own little falcon, the size of a hen. It looks tiny next to my Snow-Jer. After flying them, our keeper returned them to their cages. The two rabbits Snow-Jer captured were skinned by the cook then roasted over a campfire for our meal. After we ate, Clotaire led us on a walk. The only armor he wore was a long-sleeved shirt of chain mail and a sword strapped to his side. When I stand next to him, I come to his shoulders. My eyes are drawn to his face, which is friendly and often looking toward <u>me</u>. We were on a path leading into the woods when from up ahead we heard Petra scream.

Clotaire the Strong ran to her, his sword ready. My sister was standing on a wide log that formed a bridge over the stream. She pointed down into the water at something large and shiny. It appeared to be a huge fish, but was not moving. Clotaire waded in up to his hips for a better look. He touched the object with his foot, then turned it over. When he did, Petra and I gasped.

It was the body of a knight in full armor. Clotaire dragged him to shore.

"This man has been lost since last night," he told us after removing the helmet and recognizing the face. "We all worried when his horse returned to our encampment without him." Clotaire rolled the body onto the dry grass. Petra and I helped remove the iron leggings and shirt. No wounds or blood. I remembered having seen him at my ceremony, an older man with a deep scar across his cheek. He had smiled at me as if he were my own dear uncle.

"What happened?" Petra asked. She took the wreath of daisies from her hair and laid it on the body.

The chevalier had gone for a ride after supper, Clotaire told us, and must have fallen from his horse crossing the stream. It is shallow here, but someone dressed in heavy armor would sink like a stone.

I have ordered a hero's burial. This good man should be honored because he was prepared to give his life for mine.

Early October
Still in Cognac

The warm days become cooler by afternoon and frosty at night. Our vineyards are being harvested. In years past I have watched the villagers stomp the grapes into the juice that becomes wine. The monks have used recipes of old, storing the liquid in barrels as tall as myself, in cool cellars. It takes years for the wine to age to a perfect, rich flavor.

In the coming days we will pack up our wagons and travel north, home to Poitiers. We follow the Charente most of the way, so we'll be near freshwater. To my relief Father has not started a fight about Emma. His thoughts are on his pilgrimage, a few months away. Since he must travel over the Pyrenees, it would be too dangerous to leave now. These mountains soon will be buried in snow.

I am happy to have more time with him. Perhaps I can convince him to take us, too.

October 15th
Poitiers once again

Yesterday Petra and I stole away to our favorite rock by the river. It was warm until clouds hid the sun and a wind rose. Autumn is here. Soon we will need our wool kirtles.

When we walk beyond the palace walls, Clotaire the Strong accompanies us for protection, sometimes riding his horse so that he can better see around us. On days that we go hawking in the countryside he brings along several other chevaliers. These young men and our ladies enjoy one another's company. There is much flirting and laughter. I like the way Clotaire holds my elbow when we step across streams. Since finding that poor knight drowned because of his armor I have ordered everyone to take care around water. Our dresses are heavy, but not nearly so much as a suit of iron.

October 18th

Petra has named her falcon after Saint Luke. When I asked her why, what was the symbolism, she said there was none. She just liked the name Luke.

A shrieking storm is upon us. During chapel this morning, rain pelted in through the high window, forming puddles on the floor below. I prayed that the Spider would be content with having Emma for his wife and leave Father alone. Also that I would never again set eyes on the cur Lezay.

It is late now. Willie's suit of armor is still in the hallway near my chamber. During the four months we were gone, a mouse made a nest in the helmet. I cleaned out the wads of straw and fur, and once again have a safe hiding place for my diary.

Father has been hunting with his men. Their arrows brought down twenty-three deer, untold birds, and a bear in its den. Its thick dark fur will make a warm rug.

October 28th, feast of Saint Jude, Patron of the hopeless

After Mass this morning Father spoke to me of things in his heart. We were walking inside, through the long gallery between towers. This is the only way to take exercise when rain has us trapped within the palace walls. Some of the servants' children were playing with a ball, rolling it back and forth and trying to jump over it. Their laughter echoed up to the tall ceilings and gave Father and me a chance to talk without being heard.

He said that his prayers to Saint Jude have been answered. The thought of dying no longer fills him with hopelessness. He will be in Heaven and we, Petronilla and I, will have a good future. A letter he wrote yesterday is on its way to King Louis VI. Father turned to me and put his hands on my shoulders.

"Eleanor," he said, "if I die unexpectedly, you will be a ward of the king. Though he lives in Paris, he will take care of you and see that you marry well."

There it was again: talk of him dying. I could not speak for the lump in my throat. Why do we have to think of such things when all is going so nicely?

"But what if he refuses?" I asked.

My father laughed. "Oh, he will not refuse, *ma fille*. A

friendship between our two families is wise for both."
Father reminded me that we own more land than the king
himself. Louis the Fat will gladly see to my physical safety
so that I am not kidnapped like Emma. He can shield me
from a fortune hunter who would marry me.

October 31st

I am in my window seat, writing against my knees. A deer
hide hanging over the opening keeps the wind out, but
still I am wrapped in a wool shawl because of drafts. A
torch in the corner of the room casts a warm glow up the
walls. I'm thinking about my last talk with Father. He did
not tell me if his letter to the king said anything about
<u>who</u> should be my husband. It will be weeks before there's
any response from the royal court.

Tomorrow is All Saints' Day, to honor martyred
Christians. The feast will carry on into the wee hours. I
intend to wear a white gown with Mother's pearl necklace
and earrings. On each finger I will wear one gold band,
eight in all. Petra will probably try to copy me.

I wonder what Louis the Younger, King Louis's son,
thinks about when he looks out his castle window.

Later

Madame brought heated wine for me to drink before bed. It seemed odd, but she was out of breath from climbing the stairs. Her face was puffy, and her dress draped over her in loose folds. She was not wearing Mother's jeweled belt.

"Are you ill?" I asked. To myelf I thought, <u>All the feasts have made her fat.</u>

She smiled and rested her hand on her stomach. "No, m'lady. I am in my sixth month."

Madame is having a baby!

November 12th

I am never speaking to my sister again!

This afternoon when I was coming upstairs after a walk in the courtyard, I turned down a hallway. In the torchlight I saw someone standing next to Willie's suit of armor, reading this diary. It was Petronilla! I grabbed it from her and slapped her face.

November 18th

It is hard to stay mad at my sister. She is my best friend. Before bed last night, when I was washing my face in the basin, she came and stood next to me, crying. I hugged her, my wet hands on her back. It was then I decided to do something for her.

Clotaire the Strong escorted me through the cold fields, down to the abbey by Saint Radegund's convent. I wore my heavy cloak and a wimple to keep the wind off my neck.

Several monks were bent over tables with pens and parchment. These tables are in alcoves near windows. Because glass is so costly, the openings are instead covered by shavings from a sheep's horn, woven together like a mat. This keeps rain and wind from ruining their papers, but allows in a golden light. Most are copying Holy Scripture to make more Bibles.

I asked Brother Jean-Pierre to sew a diary for my sister with a cover of leather, not fur. And on the front to please etch a drawing of her with her falcon, Luke.

"In a matter of days, m'lady," he said, "it will be done."

December 6th, feast day of Saint Nicholas, Patron of children

This morning, to honor Saint Nicholas, Petra and I exchanged gifts. I had wrapped her diary in a blue linen cloth, tied with red string. She was so thrilled, she hurried away to a window seat in the library to begin writing. "Thank you, thank you!" she said at least ten times.

After supper I wandered by her chamber and was surprised that she had left her diary unguarded. It was on the floor by the side of her bed, for all to see! I picked it up and opened the pages. Her handwriting was in block script with curlicues at the beginning of each sentence. Quickly, I closed the book.

The worst would be for <u>her</u> to catch <u>me</u> reading.

Later, another thought

Now it is late, time to undress for bed. Petra asked me about Saint Nicholas, so I told her the story again: He lived during the fourth century and was orphaned as a young man. Because he had a generous heart, he used his inheritance for charity. He loved helping people in need. One particular merchant lost all his money. When Nicholas heard that the man's three daughters would never be able to marry because they had no dowries, Nicholas decided to do something. Secretly, in the middle of the night, he dropped a bag of gold into the open window of the family's cottage. Weeks later, after the first daughter married, Nicholas did the same for the second, then the third daughter. Some people claim that miracles have happened after touching his relics, that is, his bones. I do not know if they are buried in a tomb or are in tiny boxes scattered around the world like those of other saints.

These boxes are called reliquaries. Grandmère said there are even reliquaries holding splinters from the cross upon which Jesus was crucified. Pilgrims go to look at them and pray.

Petronilla's gift for me was one of her embroideries sewn into a purse. Its strap is woven from strips of blue and purple silk. It is pretty. I am touched that she used my favorite colors.

December 25th, first day of Christmas

The palace is decorated with boughs of pine from our forest. Servants have loaded the fireplace in the great hall with our Yule log. It is as thick as an old tree. Its warm blaze should last through the Twelfth Night, though the rest of the castle will be freezing. The rain of this morning has turned to sleet. Throughout the day gusts of wind blew down the chimney, splattering ash and soot. Some rushes caught fire when a glowing coal rolled under a table. It was quickly stamped out, but not before igniting the hem of a lady's dress. She was terribly burned about the legs, but she lives.

December 26th, second day of Christmas

We will feast and make merry Christmas for another eleven nights. This afternoon Clotaire the Strong escorted Petra and me into the village with baskets filled with bread and sweetmeats. We had spent the morning stringing dried pears and apples into small wreaths — these we hung around the necks of the girls who ran alongside our cart. Alas, I was distressed to see that many had not even a shawl to cover their heads, nor shoes. Their feet were bound with dirty rags. The wind was so cold I could barely stand it.

January 1st, eighth day of Christmas
A new year, 1137

Four more nights until Christmas is over. These are the
darkest, coldest days of winter. This is why Father makes
sure that the great hall is bright with torches and firelight,
and that at dinner the tables are heaped with hot food. Each
afternoon he visits areas of Poitiers to give out bread and
woolen scarves knit by our ladies. He has not quarreled
with anyone for weeks, but still there are whispers. It makes
me sad that people do not trust his changed heart.

January 5th, twelfth day of Christmas

Late . . . before bed . . . I am glad Christmas will be over tomorrow. After so many days of feasting and cheer, I am ready
for quiet. The best thing about this holiday is that Petra and
I get to wear a different gown each night. I know vanity is a
sin, and I am sorry to be vain, but I am also being honest. It
is the Aquitaine way, to dress in bright colors with plenty of
jewels. I do like the feeling when all eyes are upon us.

Tonight my gown was blue with a purple kirtle and
full sleeves that swept the floor when I danced. My shoes
were soiled by evening's end because the rushes were

filthy. Twelve days of people spilling wine and tossing greasy pork bones over their shoulders have left a soggy stink. Tomorrow the hall will be raked clean so that new straw can be spread out.

Grandmère gave me an exquisite ruby ring. It has a delicate gold chain that falls across the back of my hand and connects to a matching bracelet. When knights bow to me, I extend this hand for them to kiss. I cannot keep my eyes off the pretty jewels. Petronilla says that when the men kneel, she can't keep <u>her</u> eyes off the tops of their heads. Some are baldies, but most have bugs crawling through their hair: lice and fleas.

I wonder if my sister records these observations in her diary. Every evening she is busy by candlelight, writing. How I would love to have a look!

January 13th, feast of Saint Hilary, Bishop of Poitiers

This saint is beloved by the villagers because he was born here, though eight hundred years ago. He wrote beautiful hymns in Latin that monks still sing today.

A fierce wind tore down several trees in our courtyard. One of Father's jesters tried to walk along the fallen branches. He unfortunately slipped on a wet log and fell. He was carried into the hall and placed on a bed of rushes. The physician says the reason the jester cannot speak or move his arms is because his neck is broken. If he lives another day, it will be a miracle.

January 17th

I am crushed. Father says the pilgrimage will be too dangerous for Petra and me to come along. First, I worry about his being away for so long without us to care for him. Second, I want to touch the relics of Saint James the Greater. I would like a miracle that would make me a better person. If I truly had a good heart, I would not be so eager to read my sister's diary. And the thoughts I have had lately about Clotaire the Strong . . . Is it a sin to wish he would kiss me the next time we walk in the fields?

January 21st

Cold, gray days. The poor jester who broke his neck died this morning. He lay eight days in the hall, staring up at the rafters.

Later, more thoughts on Father's pilgrimage

There are three great holy places pilgrims visit: Rome, Jerusalem, and Santiago de Compostela. Father said he cannot go to Rome because Pope Innocent II is there — it would be like stepping into a hornet's nest because he has yet to be welcomed back into the Church. Father does not want to go to Jerusalem because the Saracens living there are ready to fight. So he must go to Spain. It is closer, south over the Pyrenees, a journey of just a few weeks. There might be bandits along the way, but he will not have jewels or money. What could they steal from him besides his walking stick?

As we talked, we stood before the fire in the great hall. He wore a long wool tunic over his shirt and leggings, like the peasants, and ankle boots. He stared into the flames when I asked why he must take such a long trip when God has already forgiven his sins.

"*Ma fille*," he said, "a pilgrimage invites a person to a life of contemplation. The hardship will humble me."

"But Father, why not visit Paris instead?" I argued that he could pray to the holy relics there, and the journey is safe enough for Petra and me to come, too. What I did not say was that I would like to meet the king's son. If Louis the Younger is a possible husband, I want to get a good look at him.

Father embraced me before taking the circular stairs to his apartment. The candle he carried cast tall shadows up the narrow walls. His last words were final: He wants to be near to one who witnessed the Resurrection of Christ.

Before bed

I am reading the historian Josephus, who wrote about the Jewish rebellion in the first century. There is much about the evil king Herod and other Romans. Very interesting, but I am slow translating. It will take months for me to finish this book. The only romance so far is about Cleopatra VII. Josephus says that Marc Antony was "a slave to his passion for her." I wonder if that is how Sir Lancelot felt about Guinevere. I hope the man I marry feels this way toward me.

January 24th

After our studies this morning, Grandmère invited us to sit by her fire. She reminded us of Saint Agnes, for this is her feast day, and how purity is a virtue that pleases God. We must take care to never go outside the palace walls without escorts. As Petra is twelve and I fourteen, we are of the ages where dishonorable men might try to steal us, such as the baron of Lezay. He and others still want to make trouble.

I thought about Emma being kidnapped and all the times my sister and I have sneaked away to our favorite rock. It is hard to obey everything I'm told. Sometimes I'd rather scream and kick my feet!

February 2nd

A happy event! Madame is in childbed with twin boys. They were born this morning at sunrise and have pink hair! Grandmère says they will be redheads like their father, who is one of our chevaliers. In their cradle they look like tiny dolls. Petra and I knelt over them and prayed for them to live. They were bathed with warm water heated in a cauldron. It will be summer before it's warm enough to unwrap them completely.

As Madame lay in bed without her face painted, I thought she as looked pretty as ever.

February 14th, feast day of the saints Valentine, two martyrs of this name

Our tutor says that hundreds of years ago a pope decided that Lupercalia should be celebrated today instead of February 15th. This was a pagan festival for lovers that was so cheerful, he wanted it moved to this saints' day so that it would have a Christian flavor. During Lupercalia young men and ladies would choose partners by closing their eyes then drawing names out of a box. For the rest of the festival the couples would flirt with each other and exchange gifts. Sometimes their courtships turned into marriage.

Petra begged Father to put two boxes in the great hall, so that everyone could draw names. But he said no. Most of the knights, ladies, and squires do not know how to write their names or read, so there would be much confusion. Instead there will be a banquet tonight with musicians and dancing. The weather is still cold, with a sharp wind. Father said he will try to make sure the hall is lit. It is the only place in the castle warm enough to relax.

February 15th

Last night after dinner a squire delivered a letter to me on a silver tray. I recognized the elegant script as Brother Jean-Pierre's and broke open the wax seal. It had been dictated to him by Clotaire the Strong, who cannot write. I nearly swooned upon reading the words. Indeed, I read them so many times that I have them memorized:

> *For Eleanor, daughter of Aquitaine, Poitou, and*
> *   Gascony —*
> *Your beauty surpasses a rose in bloom,*
> *Your kind gentleness inspires me to sing.*
> *How lovely are your eyes when they gaze into mine.*
> *I will stand by you through any storm,*
> *Carry you from any danger,*
> *Listen to any words from your lovely mouth . . .*

There is more, but I blush to record it here.

I spent an hour composing a poem in return and think it quite romantic. Clotaire cannot read, so he will need to take my letter to Brother Jean-Pierre. I wish I could peek into the abbey and see who turns red first: the knight or the monk.

February 25th

Father is preparing for his pilgrimage. It is peaceful compared to when he and Geoffrey the Handsome went to war. There are no weapons or armor. No chests of jewels or dressed-up horses. He will travel with just a few knights and a few friends, wearing the clothes on his back, walking all the way.

I have felt gloomy for days, knowing he leaves soon.

February 27th

There has been a happy turn of events: Father has decided to take Petra and me with him as far as Bordeaux. Then he will begin his long walk.

We leave tomorrow! As on a ducal progress, all our ladies will come, too. Cooks and laundry women, our musicians and falcons, Marcabru and Clotaire the Strong, Madame and her twin babies. If the road south is not too muddy, we should arrive next week.

March 1st
Cognac once again

I am writing from inside the damp walls of our palace. Everything — the floors, our clothing — feels wet from the constant rain. Fortunately, the wagons did not get stuck in the mud. We will stay here tonight, then tomorrow continue on our journey south. We are halfway to Bordeaux.

Cognac is very different from when we were here five months ago. The vineyards are bare because they have been pruned down to twisted little stumps. Everything looks dead. But it is this pruning that allows the vines to bear fruit in the summer.

The river is gray, the breeze from it icy. Despite the cold, pear trees are beginning to bloom. We can see tiny yellow daisies in sunny spots along the banks. I wish we could stay here longer, but Father is in a hurry.

March 3rd, first day of Lent
Still traveling

Morning, shortly after sunrise. Church bells are ringing in the distance. I am writing this from a garden bench while waiting for the horses to be harnessed. In moments, we will once again be on our way. We are at the manor of one of our vassals, which is where we stayed last night. The family was courteous, but not overjoyed to have fifty people surprise them for dinner. Petra and I slept in a bed with no sheets. There was only a thin blanket to throw over the straw. Once again we heard servants discussing our father. They say his pilgrimage is merely an excuse to spy on people. They believe he will return from Spain with more troops and weapons.

Meanwhile, Lent is being observed across the countryside. No marriages will take place during this time, and many are fasting as a way to honor Christ's sacrifice on the cross. I know of no one who will go entirely without food. Myself, I am giving up honey cakes. Forty days from now we will celebrate His Resurrection.

March 5th
Bordeaux

We are at our Ombrière palace. When <u>here</u> I think <u>this</u> is my favorite place. It feels as if we are on the ocean, but it is just the fresh air coming off the bay.

As soon as we approached the old Roman wall of the city, the weather felt warmer. Petra and I ran through our front courtyard, where there are tiled fountains and gardens with orange and lemon trees. Within the palace walls is a stout, rectangular keep, with our private apartments. From the roof I can see down to the Garonne River, which empties into the bay that opens up to the Atlantic. There are fishing boats with sails and the familiar aroma of salt air and fish. It seems that overnight spring is finally here.

The little twins survived their journey from Poitiers and are now four weeks old. They have become plump because their wet nurse is feeding them well. Nearly every day Petra and I visit and coo to them. We love babies. Their pink hair has turned golden red, and their eyes are blue like Madame's.

I have kept Clotaire's love poem hidden between these pages and often unfold it to again read his beautiful words. Alas, I am distracting myself from a painful thought. . . . Father leaves tomorrow morning! He wants to reach the tomb of Saint James the Greater before Resurrection Sunday.

No place yet to hide my diary.

Before bed

Later this afternoon Father took Petronilla and me up to the roof of our keep. We could see out over the countryside in all directions and to where the river twists through green fields. The wind wisped Father's hair around his face. His stubble of beard looked golden from the setting sun. He told us he will not shave until he returns from his pilgrimage.

"*Mes chères filles*," he said. My dear daughters. "You will be safe here. Our old friend Geoffrey du Loroux will look after you in my absence. As he is archbishop of Bordeaux, your safety and spiritual needs will be under his tender care."

Father pointed south, to the narrow road that wound its way through an orchard then opened up into a meadow. Far beyond, out of our sight, were the Pyrenees and the high mountain pass that is often shrouded in fog. From here the path descends into Spain, then westward to Santiago de Compostela.

"Watch for me in a few months," he said. "I will come back through those trees, singing with joy."

Petra cried when he folded us into his arms, but I kept my tears to myself.

Now it is late, my candle a puddle of wax. A breeze is coming in through the arrow slit beside my bed. I can see down to the dark river, where a boat is sailing upstream, a lantern at its helm. My companion tonight is Snow-Jer. Her tall cage sits on the floor near me. I just peeked under the drape that covers it, to say good-night. She opened one eye, then closed it again. I am as tired as she is. . . .

March 7th, fifth day of Lent

Father left with his men before sunrise. He was dressed as a pilgrim, in a coarse gray cloak with a hood. He had with him only a flask of water strapped across his chest and a walking stick. A full moon, though low in the western sky, cast enough light for them to see the path. I watched until they disappeared around a grove of trees. Just then the sun burst above the horizon and church bells began to ring. Time for Mass.

My sister and I consoled ourselves with a day in the sunny courtyard. No studies, no sewing. We listened to the birds. Servants brought out bread, cheese, and dried figs so that we could eat in the fresh air. I gave my honey cake to Petra. Snow-Jer sat on a perch by the fountain, a golden chain around her ankle so that she would not fly off.

Later, another thought

Father is traveling with an extra item. Petra and I gave him a brooch, which he pinned to his shoulder. It is in the shape of a scallop shell, a symbol for pilgrims. And to us, it is a memory of our summer by the sea. We carved our initials on the back.

The road to Compostela is crowded with travelers. They camp by the river, then leave the next morning before sunrise. I was surprised to see women making this long journey, too, many of them barefoot. The sight of them fills me with loneliness. If I were not heiress of Aquitaine, I could be walking with them. Any pilgrims who come near our gate are given fresh bread and meat by our cooks. This is something I've asked them to do.

March 17th, feast day of Saint Joseph of Arimathea

It has been almost two weeks since Father left. To keep from missing him, Petra and I busy ourselves. Every day we take turns reading aloud from Cicero in Latin, then we translate it into French. Grandmère insists we work on our tapestries as well as our manners. Conversation is an art, she says, and must be practiced daily to keep our minds alert. Yesterday she scolded me. "It is not good, Eleanor, to always gaze out at the clouds." She often catches me in a window seat, doing exactly that. I enjoy quiet moments to myself. Sometimes conversation makes me tired.

The archibishop of Bordeaux worries over us like a loyal friend. With his white hair under his bishop's hat and his long white beard, he looks like a grandfather. For now he will not let us out beyond the palace walls. Too much danger, he says. Word has spread among Father's unhappy vassals that he has left his daughters behind — the wealthiest daughters in all of France, of an age to marry. He is concerned the count of Angoulême might make trouble.

I love to hear the ringing of morning bells. The archbishop has asked us to join him daily for Mass, then again in the evenings for vespers. I am happy for these peaceful times and am comforted by prayer. The chapel reminds me of the one in Poitiers, with pigeons roosting high in the rafters. An open window lets them come and go. A small choir of monks sings beautiful praises in Latin.

This day honors Saint Joseph of Arimathea, who lived during the time of Christ and was a secret disciple. A legend says he had the cup from which Jesus drank during the Last Supper and that he took it to England. It is said to bring healing to those who touch it. King Arthur and his knights searched for the Holy Grail, but never found it. Sir Lancelot hoped to present it to Guinevere. It seems that many dream of touching a holy relic — kings, dukes, chevaliers, even myself.

Later, on another subject

I have finally found a hiding place. There is a cupboard against one of the walls in my apartment, with a drawer underneath. This is where my silk wimples of various colors are folded. When I was looking through this drawer, my fingers scraped against a piece of wood, which lifted up — a false bottom! Underneath is a shallow tray wide enough to hold my diary and a few little treasures, such as the ring and bracelet Grandmère gave me for Christmas. Because I choose my own wimples, there is no danger of the maids discovering my secret.

Meanwhile Petronilla still keeps her diary in plain view by the side of the bed. She trusts that no one will spy on her. Oh, how I would love to read her thoughts!

April 2nd

Spring has brought rain and more rain. Surely by now Father has climbed up the mountain and gone through the pass at Roncesvalles. Monks who have made this journey told us that the trail is steep and narrow, and the pass is often misty from the clouds. There is also much rain this time of year. Father is probably soaking wet. As he is traveling with only his cloak to protect him from the cold, I worry for his health. He is a duke! His hands are soft and white; he has always had a warm feather bed and servants. The next people who say that Father is just on a hunt for more soldiers, I will order them to hike up to Roncesvalles without carrying along food or shelter. Then they might see for themselves what pilgrims suffer. They will have to catch rabbits with their bare hands if they wish to eat.

After Mass this morning, the archbishop and I stood under an awning to watch the rain. A duck and her five babies were swimming in a pond that had formed in the courtyard. I asked him a question: "Does God hear me when I pray . . . does He care?"

"Yes, Eleanor, He cares. He knows when every sparrow falls, and are we not more important to Him than the birds? Do not worry about your papa. God knows what he needs."

Then I asked if Christ truly heals a person after a pilgrimage.

He answered, "If you do not walk with Him on the way, you will not find Him at the end of your journey."

His answers brought me comfort. I am certain Father has Christ in his heart and is indeed walking with Him toward Santiago de Compostela.

Next day

There was much crying today in the kitchen. I came upon the cook's young daughter, who hid herself in her mother's skirt, weeping. When I asked about the matter, it took some moments before I could understand her words. It seems the child had carried her kitten up to the roof, to show it a view of the river. When she needed to use the privy, she took the kitten with her into the nearby garderobe and set it upon the seat. It was, of course, curious. Stretching its neck toward the hole, it unfortunately tumbled down the long stone shaft. A worker later found it in the waste pit, but the poor thing had drowned. I have ordered that small children are to use chamber pots, unless someone is with them in a garderobe to watch for their safety. I am thankful it was not the girl who fell in.

The shaft narrows near the bottom, so it would have been impossible to rescue her.

April 4th

Seven more days of Lent. I am still fasting honey cakes. I have stopped missing them. The archbishop says that any day now Father should reach the tomb of Saint James the Greater. I rejoice for him.

Daily, we see pilgrims on the road to Compostela.

Madame brought word today that the baron of Lezay was seen in the village with the count of Angoulême. What are they doing here? Lezay is supposed to be taking care of our castle at Talmont.

April 9th, Good Friday

I do not know why they call this day "good" if it is when Jesus was crucified. Petra, who has been faithfully reading the Gospels, explained her thoughts to me. She sat with me in our window seat this morning. She smoothed the layers of her skirt over her folded knees and opened her Bible. Usually I do not take kindly to my little sister instructing me, but today she spoke with such sincerity that I listened.

"The day is good," she said, "because it is the beginning of the best news ever given. Jesus predicted His own death, then told the disciples that after three days in the grave He would come back to life. . . ."

Before Petra could finish, Grandmère interrupted us for a light meal, served in the hall. No music. No jesters or dancing. Drapes have darkened the windows so that the only light is from torches. The darkness is gloomy to me. Thinking of the Roman soldiers nailing Jesus to a cross . . . I cannot bear it. I had my repast served to me here, where at least I can look out the arrow slits for sky and sunshine. For some reason my heart is heavier today than in years past.

April 11th, Sunday

He is risen!

At sunrise, church bells rang and rang, celebrating the Resurrection of Christ. During the Mass, Petra kneeled beside me on the stone floor. We understood the priest's Latin, but it is much prettier in French. I translate it here:

On this day so many years ago, the disciples were in a house with the doors locked because they feared the authorities. They were grieving the death of Jesus. Suddenly, He appeared in the room. "Peace be with you!" Jesus said. Then He breathed on them and said, "Receive the Holy Spirit!"

James the Greater was there in that room with the holy apostles. That is why our father is walking so many leagues to touch his tomb.

April 13th

Rain still. Before noon, Petra came into the library, where I was studying. The light is better here because of the alcoves. She brought several books to our seat and began reading. What happened next was truly an accident. I did not plan it.

She fell into a light sleep. When she laid her head back onto a cushion, the books in her lap slid to the floor. One fell open near me, so I could see the pages.

It was her diary.

My eyes fell on her neat handwriting. I could not keep myself from reading. It was a poem about the kitten that fell down the garderobe, and what it must have been like to swim in the waste pit. Petra was descriptive to the point that my stomach felt queasy. At the bottom of the second page she had begun another poem. It was about one of the knights who smiles at her all the time, a whisper, a kiss. . . . But alas, I would have had to turn the page to know more.

Was this just her imaginings, or did something happen? I could not bring myself to pick up her diary to read further. If she discovered my deed, Petra would never again trust me.

I stayed in our seat for some time, tortured that my sister's secrets were an arm's length away and that she was sound asleep. At last I laid my own head back on a pillow and closed my eyes. It was thus we spent this rainy afternoon.

April 14th

Madame brought her babies to the courtyard this morning, for finally there was sunshine. A blanket was spread under an orange tree so that they could lie on their backs and look up through the branches at blue sky. The sweet aroma of orange blossoms filled the air.

Before sunset I walked along the rooftop of our keep. The view of the river and surrounding countryside filled me with longing. How I yearn to be beyond these walls!

To ride horseback wherever the path might take me. . . . I want to go hawking with Snow-Jer, without someone watching her in the sky to learn my whereabouts on the ground below. It is hard for me to believe that my life is in such danger.

I looked down at the silvery blue strip of water that is the Garonne. One year Father sailed with us down this river into the bay that opens up to the ocean. I remember the water was choppy. The wind filled the sails with such force our boat heeled onto its side, slicing through the swells that were topped with foam. It was thrilling, but Father soon turned back. Petronilla and I had become sick because we were not used to the waves. It is a day I will never forget. That is what I think about when I watch the fishing boats sail out to sea: being with Father.

It has been sunny and warm for several days now. I hope he is having the same pleasant weather.

April 17th

Father has been gone six weeks. I wish I had asked how long he planned to stay at Santiago de Compostela. If for only a short while, then he is probably now on his way home. I have begun looking out toward the southern road three times a day. After morning bells, at noon, then just before sunset. Petra stands with me on the roof. We see pilgrims, but they are all walking toward Spain.

I am still wondering about her love poem, but do not know how to ask her without revealing that I read her diary!

April 23rd, feast of Saint George the Dragon Slayer

Another banquet is planned for this evening. I am in the mood for dancing and music and poetry! Marcabru told us he has written new songs, and our jesters are eager to show new tricks they've learned. I hope that when they are somersaulting off tables, they are careful not to hurt themselves.

Here at our Ombrière palace there is a tapestry hanging in the great hall. It is a beautiful scene of Saint George slaying the dragon. I like the picture of the maiden standing safely behind him.

Before the banquet

Petra and I are dressed in matching gowns, though mine is violet, hers silver. We have new dancing slippers, which means they are plain silk. I do not wish to cut my ankles again from the rubies sewn into my other shoes. It is unpleasant to have blood stain my hem.

Oh . . . we can hear horsemen coming across the drawbridge. Petra has run to the window to look out and is shouting with excitement.

"Couriers!"

Later, near midnight

I am writing by torchlight in my apartment. Petra is here with me. We cannot sleep.

The messengers who arrived before sunset were taken to the archbishop's office. We hurried down the hallway and knocked on the thick wooden door. He opened it to say that we would speak in the morning. I stood on my toes to look behind him, to see the men who had come from afar. I saw only their knees and muddy boots, for they were sitting on a bench to the side.

"Now enjoy your banquet, *mesdemoiselles*," he said. "Morning will come soon enough."

It was hard to be festive. We could not find Grandmère, and the absence of Archbishop du Loroux made me believe that something dreadful had happened.

When the lutes and tambourines began playing, Petra and I felt cheered enough to dance. We circled the room with the other ladies and squires, our arms bent at our sides to swirl our long sleeves. Marcabru sang to me his song about Clotaire the Strong, who dined at our table. Then he sang to Petronilla about her knight, who also sat with us. I did not blush as I would have another time, because my thoughts were elsewhere. Something serious was being discussed upstairs, and I feared it concerned us.

Now my sister and I are wide awake. Grandmère still has not come in to say good-night, nor has Madame visited us with any news. Petra is about to use the garderobe. When she leaves, I will slip my diary into the secret drawer.

A footman has just come in to transfer the torch to the hallway. Alas, the room will soon be dark. . . . I shall close these pages.

May 2nd

It has been nine days since the messengers came. I have put off writing the terrible news, because my heart is broken.

Father is dead.

Petra and I cannot believe it.

The men who rode into our courtyard had met Father's friends on the mountain pass of Roncesvalles. The friends had been running for days, from Santiago de Compostela, and were so exhausted that they had collapsed by the side of the road. They had been trying to hurry home to Bordeaux, to relay their sad news. The men on horseback were kind enough to complete the journey for them.

When at last Archbishop du Loroux came to us, his face was pale. It looked as if he had not slept all night. In his hand he held a cloth, bundled up and tied with a long blade of grass. He handed it to me. I unwrapped it to find that it was Father's shirt. Pinned to it was the scallop shell we had given him. There was a note:

> *Most cherished daughters,*
> *When you receive this do not weep, for you*
> *must know that I am filled with joy. I am only one*
> *day's walk from Saint James the Greater, though it*

will be my friends who walk, taking turns carrying me upon their shoulders. Dear children, I am ill. Unfortunately, my hunger did not afford wisdom, for I ate a fish before cooking it properly. Now I am dying from its poison. A traveler has given me this paper and ink so that I could write to you in my own hand. If I do not return to you, just know that we shall meet again in paradise.

Your loving Father

On Good Friday his friends arrived at Santiago de Compostela and carried him into the chapel. I do not know if it was actually a tomb he touched or a reliquary filled with assorted bones, but Father died shortly after. They buried him near the high altar. He was thirty-eight years of age.

I wept upon hearing this, wishing he had been healed of the poison. I cried out to God. It wasn't fair that Papa traveled all that way just to die. I buried my face in his shirt and would not be consoled. Petronilla put her arms around me. She said into my ear, "But Eleanor, he <u>has</u> been healed. In heaven there are no more tears or sorrow, no illness or pain. . . ."

Even so, as I write these words, I am not comforted.

May 3rd

There is other news.

The archbishop paid the horsemen to deliver an urgent message. They are now on their way to Paris to see the king, Louis the Fat. It is a brief letter, just eight words:

> *Duke William is dead. Eleanor must marry*
> *immediately.*

I asked why Father's death means I must marry right away. Archbishop du Loroux took my arm and led me to the gallery, where gray light filled the tall windows. Once again we were inside because of rain. We walked the length of the gallery several times. I kept my eyes on the tapestries that covered each wide wall. One was a hunting scene, dogs chasing deer through a forest. The other showed King Arthur with his knights. Up to one end we walked, then turned around and back to the other end. It is a good way to take exercise on wet days.

The archbishop kept his hands behind his back, thoughtful. His bishop's hat was like a dark dome over his white hair. He reminded me that I am now duchess of Aquitaine and Gascony, and countess of Poitou. All this land is now my responsibility to oversee. I am a prize in the eyes of many men, he said, but few are worthy of being my husband. I asked whom the king would pick.

He chuckled, then looked over at me. "My dear, he will choose his own son, of course: Louis the Younger."

"Are you sure?"

"I am positive," he said. "With you as his daughter-in-law, the king of France will finally have more land than all his vassals. Only a fool would ignore this opportunity, and Louis the Fat is no fool."

So we wait. This time Petra and I look to the north. In days or weeks horsemen should be coming from Paris with word from the king. I watch this road with a quiet heart.

At the moment I am too grieved from losing Father to also be upset by marriage plans.

May 15th

Marcabru sang an ode for Father, at a ceremony in our courtyard. It was sunny, a relief from so much rain. Seabirds circled overhead as if crying farewell to an old friend. Petronilla and I stood together with Grandmère. A lump in my throat prevented me from telling Marcabru how much his words meant to me. His song was a sincere telling of Father's good qualities, touched with sadness because he is gone.

Afterward, I climbed to the roof to feel the breeze from the river. The sight of pilgrims on the road of Compostela made me want to cry.

𝔐ay 19th

The days are warm. I often look from the rooftop down to the river and wish I could drift in a little boat. Weather like this reminds me of packing our things for Talmont-by-the-Sea. This summer will be the first that Petra and I are trapped inland. Bordeaux is beautiful, and I love it here, but it does not look out on the ocean. And Father is not here.

Three weeks since we sent word to the king.

𝔐ay 22nd

Yesterday riders from the north arrived after sunset, carrying the royal flag and bearing a letter. They were escorted by torchlight to the archbishop. This time my sister and I were allowed to hear the news right away. Our guardian took the folded piece of parchment and broke open the king's seal with his thumbnail. The sealing wax was crimson, the size of a large coin. He leaned toward a candle, read silently, then handed the message to me.

It was longer than our letter by two words:

Eleanor and Young Louis will marry this summer in Bordeaux.

Archbishop du Loroux looked at me with kind eyes. "Well, my dear, this means we must wait for the prince to arrive."

I suddenly felt short of breath. My heart was beating fast, but I did not know if it was from fear or from excitement. I think I am queasy, but from what I don't know.

This morning when I stepped outside for fresh air, Petronilla was in the garden. She sat in the shade, writing in her diary. The fountain near her was busy with tiny songbirds. They flew up and away at my approach.

Oh, how I wished my sister would drop off to sleep with the pages open! I would like to know what she thinks about my becoming a bride. Instead of tempting myself by sitting on the bench next to her, I climbed the outer stairs up to the roof. From the battlements I could see down to the moat, where a family of swans was gliding over the green water. Behind them, their wakes spread ripples to the mossy walls.

<u>Prince Louis</u>. Husband. Such a strange thought. He is almost sixteen. I try to imagine what type of boy he might be. <u>What does he think about in his quiet hours? Is he short or tall? Is he huge like his father? What color are his eyes?</u>

Grandmère has told me everything she can remember about him, but it's been several years since they met. At the time he was just a boy. She saw him ride off on a hunt with his squires, but instead of returning with a fox or deer, he had a book in his vest. A prayer book. He had spent the afternoon under a tree, reading. His father the king was not pleased. I like Grandmère's story, but I hope the prince is brave like Clotaire the Strong.

Louis and I are fourth cousins.

Later, other thoughts

We have not been able to go hawking because it is too dangerous for me to be out in the fields. Our falconer is going to summer at Talmont-by-the-Sea, where it is cooler. He will take Snow-Jer, Luke, and Father's prized birds with him.

One thought troubles me: With Lezay minding the castle, he might do something terrible to make those birds his. I do not trust him. I must think of a way to remove him as castellan.

Father tolerated his lack of respect, but I shall not.

June 4th

Two weeks since we received the letter from King Louis the Fat. As the days grow hotter, I yearn more and more for my freedom. We asked the archbishop if we could please walk along the river where it is cool. This time we would go with extra chevaliers.

He shook his head sadly. "You are even more valuable, now that you are to be married to the prince of France. The stakes are too high. Your life could end up as ransom for any number of ruthless men." He took my hands in his. "Please do not ask me again, Eleanor."

I lowered my head in respect and vowed to myself that I would keep my sorrows quiet. I could see that it was difficult for our friend to refuse me.

June 11th

The twins are four months old. Petra and I spent the day with them in the garden, taking turns holding one, then the other. We cannot tell them apart, for their faces are as alike as their downy red hair and blue eyes. Madame whispers stories to them about their brave father, chevalier to the duke of Aquitaine.

The sun beating down on the stones in the courtyard is hot, so workers made an open-air tent for us. It is strips of blue silk sewn together into a canopy large enough to shade twenty of us. It is the nearest thing to being out in the marketplace. We play checkers on small tables, and chess. How I love to move the knights around on the board, to protect their queen. It has become a passion of mine now, playing chess. It is a pleasure to pretend that I need only skill to survive. No blood is shed in our garden.

June 21st, Midsummer's Eve

This is my favorite day of the year, the middle of summer. From the roof we watched villagers celebrate with bonfires and singing. As the sky grew dark, my sister and I had our own entertainments up there. We danced with our ladies while our minstrels played drums and tambourines. We removed our wimples so that our hair could blow free. It felt wonderful . . . the closest thing to running by myself along the shore.

June 28th

Messengers on swift horses arrived today from the north. They said that Louis the Younger left Paris on June 18th. With him are five hundred knights on horseback, scores of servants, and dozens of baggage carts pulled by more horses. The summer's heat is fierce, so they rest during the day and travel by night. I wonder how many torches it will take to light their way when the moon is low. The trip will take one month because there are so many people and animals.

The messengers said that a treasure chest of jewels is hidden in one of the wagons and is for me. It is still hard to believe I will soon be a wife. <u>And</u> a princess. Would this please Father, that I am to marry into the royal family?

I do hope the king's men are well armed and that their helmets do not hinder their vision. The archbishop told me that bandits live in the forests along the road from Paris to Bordeaux. They think nothing of killing for gold or kidnapping a bride. Sometimes they will even rob pilgrims of their cloaks, just to be cruel.

Madame said they are riding through the lands of the count of Angoulême.

June 30th

Our Ombrière palace is a good fortress. No one can enter who is not supposed to. Nor can I get out. If I sit by the fountain in the courtyard, close my eyes, and listen to the splash of water, I can pretend the river is nearby.

I have had just a few weeks to realize that I will never see my father again. And even less time to realize I shall soon be married. To a prince! Petra came into my apartment this morning to find me weeping on my bed. When she tried to comfort me, I couldn't tell her what was wrong because I did not know.

Then during dinner I burst into hysterical laughter as Marcabru was singing. The room dropped into silence, and all eyes turned my way. The song was not comical; it was about King Arthur's search for the Holy Grail. People do not laugh at this story; they get tears. Whatever is the matter with me?

Later, more thoughts on marriage

Grandmère took me up to the ramparts tonight, where we could look out over the darkened countryside. Specks of moving light showed where knights walked with torches around our castle. The stars were brilliant. We listened to the music of a far-off harp, then when it stopped, we listened to the quiet. The night was so still. A faint breeze brought coolness to the stone battlements, still warm from the hot summer day.

My dear grandmother said she had taught me everything I would need to know about being a princess. My manners would bid me well at the king's table. And my conversation would surely charm any royals who meet me.

"Remember the curtsy, my dear, and never, ever turn your back on the king. Walk several paces behind the queen, never alongside her."

I could see Grandmère's face in the starlight. She looked over at me with a smile, a tear on her wrinkled cheek. For the first time since I was a child, she pulled me into her arms.

July 1st

How long the days seem! It is cool within the palace's thick walls, but I get so tired of being inside that when the sun finally begins to set, I go up to the roof. The road is still busy. It seems that some of the pilgrims who passed by in the spring are now returning home. Our cooks bake extra bread to give them, as well as fruit. I have ordered that no fish be offered to travelers, in case they are too hungry to cook it properly.

I wish Father were here to stand with us. Petronilla and I miss him. We like to look out at the villagers going to market and visiting with their neighbors. I often hear laughter — not the drunken kind, but that which makes me think of happiness. There is always music from one cottage or another.

If the people have suffered because of our father's harshness, I am truly sorry and will try somehow to make life better for them.

Later, before bed

This evening Petra told me about her chevalier. They have been exchanging letters! He cannot read, of course, but that does not bother my sister. One of the monks does the writing, then reads aloud to him her words of affection. I was silent as she told me this because I hoped she would keep talking and tell me more. She did!

I now know she dreams of marrying this knight. She has just passed her thirteenth birthday and can wed if she likes. But I do not think the archbishop will allow her to marry this man. His relatives are just farmers.

Oh yes, I am now fifteen.

We watch the northern road. There are pilgrims, but no prince.

July 3rd

Riders came across the drawbridge this afternoon with a message from Prince Louis. His caravan has stopped in Limoges, still many leagues away, but should arrive here within a fortnight. Fourteen more days until I meet him.

Preparations are being made for the wedding, though we do not know what day or where it will take place. Seamstresses have been fitting me for the bridal gown: scarlet satin to be layered over ivory skirts. Shoes of soft, white leather. I have tried them on several times and find them so comfortable that I would like to wear them every day.

Our ladies are putting together my trousseau: the many dresses, wimples, kirtles, and underthings to take into my marriage. Already twelve large trunks have been packed. Sweet-smelling lilac and rose petals have been pressed between the folded layers of cloth. Then my ladies sprinkled in shavings of cinnamon, cloves, and lemon peel. When I arrive in Paris and open the lids, this lovely scent will remind me of home.

July 7th

I awoke in the middle of the night, my heart racing, my cheeks wet. Had I been dreaming? Why was I crying?

Then I remembered.

After the wedding I am to leave Bordeaux, possibly never to return . . . beautiful Bordeaux with the little boats sailing toward the sea. Paris will be my new home. Grandmère said the royal palace is on an island in the middle of the Seine River in the middle of nowhere. Paris is leagues away from the ocean, leagues away from Aquitaine.

I will be without a single friend.

I lay back in bed, but did not sleep. The moon cast pools of light on the floor. Now it is dawn. I am writing by candle while outside the sun rises from behind the distant trees. Bells are ringing. Time for Mass . . . I will wake Petra.

Next Day

Grandmère found me in the courtyard this morning, writing in this diary. The breeze ruffled the pages when I set my pen down, and her eyes fell upon what I had written last night.

"My heavens, Eleanor, I thought you knew. You will not be alone in Paris, no, not at all."

Then she told me the happy news. At least eight of our ladies will accompany me and — best of all — Petronilla, too. My sister will be with me! I feel such relief. A heaviness has lifted from my heart.

Grandmère also described what the wedding feast would be like, the meats and cakes, our own Bordeaux wine made by the monks. Invitations are being delivered to one thousand nobles throughout Aquitaine, instructing them to arrive before the last Sunday of July.

As she spoke, I found myself holding my breath. Plans were swirling around me, people would soon be coming to wish me well, and I have yet to meet my intended husband.

July 9th

Two knights in silver armor rode through our gates this morning and said that the prince should be here any day. I paced around the garden until the heat forced me inside, where it is always cool. Then all afternoon I paced in the gallery, up to one end then back to the other. In between I have gone up to the roof several times to look north. It seems that in the distance there is dust rising from the road.

But then I remembered the caravan would not be traveling during the hot afternoon. What I saw must have been smoke from their cooking fires.

I tried to imagine hundreds of chevaliers upon their horses, coming this way. Grandmère explained that the prince did not need all these men to guard him. They were for me, for protection. The king wants to make sure I am escorted to Paris in safety.

It makes me happy to think that Father's prayers have been answered.

Midnight

Petra and I could not sleep, so we climbed the stairs in our nightdresses. A warm breeze blew our hair off our necks.

Far in the north there were pricks of light stretching for what seemed like leagues. My heart beat fast. They were torches, lighting the way for the prince.

My sister and I have been sharing the wide bed in my chamber and are now both writing in our diaries. In the center of the room there is a table with a candle. It is as tall and thick as my arm, casting good light for us to see. More than once tonight we have set down our pens and put ourselves to bed. She dozed off to be woken by <u>me</u> whispering, then I dozed and <u>she</u> woke me with whispers. It is hard to sleep! Never before have we felt such happy anticipation.

July 10th

I am in the outdoor kitchen, of all places, writing from a stool. With such hot weather, one would think it the last place to sit. But I wanted to be near the cooks I have known all my life, and their small children. They run in and out from the shaded canopy with assorted kittens and things to show me. They are mindful only of their play, not yet aware that a royal army is coming our way. Nor do they know that a prince will soon walk through this very courtyard. Their carefree laughter cheers me and helps me remember my brother, Willie. Oh, that I could be a child once more.

Midnight

The torches are nearing! Petra shook me awake, then pulled me by the arm all the way up the stairs. When I leaned out over the wall, the wind in my face made me feel as a bird might, ready to fly. We strained to listen. In the distance there was a faint rustle, like the movement of horses . . . and creaking from wagon wheels. Where in the long line of light and shadow was the prince? Could he see us, atop the jagged castle wall, the sleeves of our white gowns waving?

July 11th

I am hurriedly writing this in my apartment. After watching the torches for some time, we lowered ourselves to the floor and napped, leaning against the wall. It seems that moments later we awoke to the sound of horses whinnying, but the sun was already far above the horizon. We must have slept for hours. Petra and I jumped up to look out.

The sight took my breath away.

On the other side of the river, at the edge of the woods, a village of colorful tents had sprung to life. We could hear the ring of axes cutting wood. Smoke trailed above campfires, and the aroma of roasting meat filled the air. We saw squires unsaddling horses. Knights stripped of their shirts were wading in the river.

Because there is no bridge across this part of the river, small boats were ferrying some of the men across. They appeared to be abbots and other royal advisers. I started to wave but, to my surprise, Grandmère appeared and grabbed my arm. She was not pleased to find us on the roof in our nightclothes. She directed us to immediately go downstairs and dress properly.

So here we are. I am waiting for a maid to bring my gown — blue today, with a golden kirtle. I've heard the prince likes blue and gold. They are the colors of his family's coat of arms.

Later, a day I will never forget

It is late, after midnight; my eyes are heavy. Petra has collapsed next to me on the bed, fast asleep.

How do I describe the feeling of finally stepping out

beyond the castle walls after three long months? Perhaps it was foolhardy, but I commanded the guards at the gate to let Petra and me pass over the drawbridge. We then walked by ourselves down to the river. Grandmère and her ladies called after us to stop, but God forgive me, I did not listen. Clotaire hurried from his post to help us into a boat. In minutes, a light breeze sailed us across. My sister and I lifted the hems of our skirts to step out onto the beach.

In a meadow there was a group of jugglers and jesters. They must have been from the king's court because I did not recognize their brightly colored tunics or pointed shoes. The sight of them made me smile. Petra squeezed my hand with excitement. There was so much to take in! The sunbaked grass where we walked smelled like fresh hay. The colors and aromas filled me with unexpected pleasure.

We wanted to see what people from Paris look like — the musicians and servants, the cooks, the squires. <u>What do they wear? Do they speak with accents?</u>

It was most improper of me, but I decided to meet the prince right then, without all the nobles bowing and giving speeches. I set out toward the large blue tent with royal flags. A knight stood in front, next to a banner displaying the fleur-de-lis. <u>The prince must be inside</u>, I thought.

The path took us along the river, by a sandy beach

shaded by willows. Some boys were waist deep, splashing one another. It looked most inviting.

Suddenly I could no longer stand the heat — my dress prickled! I plunged into the cool water, up to my ribs, Petra behind me. Our skirts floated up and around us as if we were sitting on lily pads. It felt divine. How I wanted to dunk my head and drift away.

A man's frantic voice startled me. I turned toward shore to see Archbishop du Loroux hurrying our way, his arms in the air. "Eleanor!" he cried. "What in God's name are you doing?"

One of the boys in the river waded over to us. He took our hands, leading us out of the current. I should say he <u>pulled</u> us, because our dresses were so soggy we were having difficulty taking a step.

When the archbishop reached us, his face was red from the effort. "My dear," he said, "your grandmother would faint to see you like this. But since we're here, allow me to introduce you to his royal highness, Prince Louis Capet of France." He bowed toward the boy who had helped us.

No one was more surprised than I. We stared at each other while standing in the shallow water. This was the prince? His bare chest was tanned, and his hair curled to his shoulders. He was tall. I don't remember the color of his eyes, only that they were gentle.

He smiled at me. "M'lady, they told me to expect a spirited one, but they did not say this is how we would meet." He took my hand and kissed my fingers.

I was without words! Was I supposed to curtsy to a prince? Had Grandmère taught me this, but I had not listened? Oh . . . my candle is going! I have so much more to write. . . .

July 12th

This is a curious thing, but the Parisians have heavy accents! They speak rapidly and use phrases I've never heard before. When the royal advisers talk, it sounds as if they are spitting through their noses. The prince said my accent was quaint, that he could tell I was raised in the south. Petra and I exchanged glances, for we know we do not have accents. They do.

No matter. Our meeting continued in the river. A crowd gathered. I could hear people whispering about us, the duchess and the prince. Archbishop du Loroux grew nervous and tried to usher us onto the bank, but I did not want to step back into the hot sun. Poor Archbishop du Loroux. I do not make his task easy.

Meanwhile my sister grew tired of waiting, so she sat

down on the bank. She picked up stones and began building a little castle in the mud. Though she seemed busy, I knew she was listening carefully to everything we said.

Petra and I are in bed now. She is propped up against the cushions and writing away madly in her diary. I want so much to read what she thinks, but whenever I lean close to her, she covers the page with her elbow. She makes me angry.

July 15th

The wedding is ten days from now! Archbishop du Loroux will perform the ceremony in the cathedral of Saint-André. Afterward everyone will come here, to Ombrière palace, for the final banquet.

I say "final" because every night since the prince arrived, there have been feasts and festivities, much like Christmas. By the time I am married, people will be calling this the Twelve Days of Eleanor's Wedding!

Banquets begin each morning and last until midafternoon, when most guests fall asleep from too much food and wine. Then at sunset, when people wake up again, the evening's entertainment begins. Troubadours stroll by the tables, singing old songs and making up new ones when they see something that amuses them. Minstrels also wander about, playing music on their lutes and tambourines, harps and flutes. I can tell when one of our jesters has told a vulgar joke because women will shriek and cover their mouths while the men explode with laughter. While all this is going on, acrobats leap and somersault over one another in their brightly colored costumes. The crowd always breaks into applause at the sight of Father's dwarf. He rides into the room on a hunting dog, blowing a little trumpet, his saddle adorned with bells.

The head table is at one end of the great hall, raised a foot higher than all the others. This way we can see everyone. Louis and I sit next to each other, his advisers on his side, mine on my side. This means, of course, Petronilla, Grandmère, the archbishop, and Madame. How I wish Father and Mother were here! They would be happy to see such a cheerful gathering, all to honor the marriage of their firstborn.

The tables are crowded with ladies and lords. Every few minutes a cluster of them will come up to me, curtsy or bow, then introduce themselves. We exchange pleasantries. If they hold grudges against Father, they do not show it. I keep glancing through the crowd for the familiar faces of the Spider and Lezay. Would they dare show themselves here?

The voices of hundreds of guests are so loud that Louis

and I must shout to hear each other. He seems shy, for when I asked him his opinion of Marcabru's poems, he rubbed his chin as if trying to think of the right thing to say.

"Well," he said, "we are not accustomed to such — how does one say it? — such passion."

To myself I thought, <u>Marcabru, passionate?</u> He sings of love and romance, of Lancelot and Guinevere. We are used to this.

July 17th, eight days until the wedding

Louis wears a different-colored shirt each night. Velvet with bell sleeves, and a thick gold chain at his throat. His hair is the color of sand, his eyes green. I like the way he smiles at me, but I am unable to return his affection. I don't know why.

While we're at the table, servants stand behind our chairs. They are taught to watch for our every need, but to be silent unless spoken to. I am sure they listen to every word we say. When they return to the kitchen, they confide to their friends, who confide to <u>their</u> friends. Soon a simple dinner conversation becomes palace gossip.

I wish Louis and I could have a few moments alone, to speak privately, but it seems it won't be allowed until our wedding night. At this evening's banquet we were more at ease with each other. This time he spoke first. He asked if all the Aquitaine women were so carefree. He nodded toward the dancers, whose bracelets clinked with the movements of their arms. Their dresses were flowing silk. Many of the ladies wear low-cut gowns to show off their bosoms.

He said, "The clothing and jewelry is — how shall I say it? — more bold than what we see in Paris."

I turned away from him, not sure how to answer. What did he mean, <u>more bold</u>? I had a sinking feeling that Louis did not know how to enjoy himself. Will life with his royal family be dull? I excused myself from the table and hurried away; my loyal sister followed. Our footsteps rang over the stone hallway and up the stairs. When we reached our chamber, I burst into tears.

"No one will like me in Paris," I cried. "They will make fun of my accent and what I wear."

Now Petra and I are in our window seat. Outside there are torches lighting the garden. We can hear music from downstairs, and laughter. I wish I felt as lighthearted as everyone else. Not since Mother died have I wept so.

Petra turned away from the window to look at me. Her braids were atop her head tonight, with daisies woven in like a floral crown.

"Don't worry, Eleanor," she said. "I know you will make the best of things."

Next morning

The summer's heat makes me drowsy, even at this early hour. I am sitting in a small private garden off the court-yard in the shade of a pear tree. The gate is hidden under a tangle of vines, so few people know how to get in. A foun-tain splashes into a tiled pool where we cool our feet. It is the only place we can come to be alone (besides the garde-robe). Meanwhile the windows high above us are open to the great hall, where the banquet has begun. I cannot bear another day of noise and giddiness. . . . It is impossible to think! And I want to think.

Prince Louis Capet.

He is kind to me, he is pleasant looking, but he seems as mild as a monk. I must stop comparing him to Clotaire the Strong. Grandmère reminded me that my duty is to marry the king's son whether I like him or not.

"Someday, you may love each other," she said. "First, you become friends."

I will try not to be offended by what the prince says about our customs.

July 19th, six days until the wedding

Unpleasant news is being whispered through the palace.

One of the king's advisers, Abbot Suger, came to Louis and me at dinner, kneeling on the floor between us. He waved away our servants.

"The count of Angoulême wants to start trouble," he said. Once again the Spider is stirring up other nobles who hate my family. Abbot Suger is worried they will try to make trouble after our wedding, when we leave the safety of this castle. He says that as a princess I will be worth a fortune. Someone might try to steal me for a royal ransom.

I searched Louis's face as he listened. He nodded, but otherwise showed no emotion.

"Eleanor," he said after the abbot left us. He leaned so close to me, I felt his breath against my ear. "We must plan an escape. We will have to outsmart these old enemies of your father's."

I smiled at him, for the first time since our meeting in the river.

July 21st, four days until the wedding

Do I dare say I am excited to be wed? Louis and I were together yesterday afternoon . . . alone!

After Abbot Suger left our table the other night, I told Louis about a secret place to meet. Thereupon, yesterday we waited until the morning's feast was well over. When the guests and nobles and advisers had wandered off to doze in whatever bit of shade they could find, Louis and I went separate ways, to meet later.

My dear sister and Madame coaxed Grandmère into the library's cool alcove, where they would read aloud to one another. Then I hurried to my garden.

I was almost trembling while waiting for the prince to arrive. To refresh myself I dipped my hands into the fountain and splashed my face. When at last I heard footsteps on the gravel, I peered out through the fence. It was he, dressed in black shirt and pants, with a purple tunic. He came quickly to the gate, then stooped through the opening I made by parting the vines. This time I returned his smile. He took my hand and led me under the tree's wide branches so that we could sit in the shade.

"How did you get away?" I asked.

He laughed. "Garderobe. But someone will come looking soon."

So we spoke quickly. We planned how we would escape the count of Angoulême, but what else we said to each other, I don't remember. I do remember, though, how he looked at me. At first he was timid, but as the minutes passed he began to say words of endearment. "Eleanor, you are — how does one say it? — lovely, so lovely." I leaned forward to hear him better, hoping he would say more, but voices from the other side of the garden wall silenced us. People were looking for the prince.

And Archbishop du Loroux was looking for me. I could hear the anxiety in his voice. "A maiden must protect her virtue," he was saying to someone. This is why Petra and I are not allowed to be alone with a man until we marry.

By the time Louis slipped out of the garden, I realized we had not spoken of our wedding! I watched through the vines as he joined his surprised advisers in the courtyard. He did not give away our hiding spot by even a glance backward.

Late

Petra is here with me, whispering into the wee hours. It is long past midnight. We are lying in bed under a comforter.

Though it is summer, it is always cool within our castle walls.

I was so pleased that she distracted Grandmère this afternoon, I told her everything Louis and I said. She threw her arms around my neck and cried, "Oh, isn't it wonderful . . . you're going to be a princess!"

July 23rd

Now I suffer from worry. In just two days we will be married. The cooks and bakers are frantically busy. I saw some of the cakes. Already there are dozens stacked on narrow trestles in the cellar. They will be decorated with honeycombs shaped into miniature castles and other scenes. Everyone in the palace is hurrying about. Because we have so many guests, our laundry women are working hard to wash the soiled clothing that is brought down to them. How they know what belongs to whom is a mystery to me. Ropes stretched along the side of our keep are where they hang shirts and billowy skirts out to dry. The yard looks like a festival of colored flags.

During our banquet this morning I turned to Louis and excused myself. Not because I was upset, but because the noise was making my head ache. He squeezed my hand as I stood to leave. A servant pulled back my chair for me.

I hurried up to the roof to feel the breeze on my face. I will miss looking out over the Garonne River and watching the fishing boats sail out to sea. I will miss the cobbled streets of Bordeaux, though I've not been able to walk upon them, only observe from above. Will it be easier to be a princess in Paris than it was to be a duchess here? Will a royal army escort me each time I want to take a walk?

The secret drawer where I hide this diary is being emptied today so that the wimples can be packed in my remaining trunks. But I have a new place. When Louis presented me with a strand of pearls, I was pleased most of all with the small chest they came in. It fits easily on my lap. When the lid opens, it lies flat, so I use it for a writing desk. Inside will go my ink flask, quills, and these writings, with a gold lock keeping it secure. I wear the key around my neck on a long string inside my shift.

In a few days I will come to the end of this diary. Perhaps one of the monks will make a new one, for I would like to record what it is like to meet the king, and what the queen looks like, her style of dress, those sorts of matters. Petra will soon need another one as well.

July 24th, the wedding is tomorrow!

In a few minutes Grandmère will show me how to walk during the ceremony and what my vows will be. Petra will stay at my side through it all. My gown is a brilliant red with pearls sewn along the neckline and sleeves. A robe of the same color has a hood with white fur. I would enjoy its warmth in winter, but it will be miserable on a hot July day.

From the roof this afternoon I saw villagers making ready for my wedding. They are hanging garlands and colorful banners from their upstairs windows. The palace cooks will come out into the streets to share tables of roasted meats, cakes, and wine. No wonder the people are happy about tomorrow.

July 25th . . . Today we wed!

I am up early. The church bells are ringing for Mass, but I shall stay here this morning, in my cool chamber. In a few hours Louis and I will ride to the cathedral of Saint-André. I am excited beyond words, and anxious. I pray the plans we made will not be discovered by the count of Angoulême.

Petra has just brought me a bouquet of flowers she picked in the garden. I shall carry them with me to breathe in their sweetness as we pass the foul odors of the streets. Oh . . . Grandmère calls . . . the ladies are here to help me dress! I hope to have time later to record everything that happens this day.

After sunset

I am writing from a tent in the woods, by the light of a small candle. Petra and I are alone; our ladies are next to us in another tent. For our protection, soldiers from the king's army surround us. The murmur of their voices is soothing to me. I can hear crickets, also the river . . . its splashes remind me of the fountains at Ombrière palace. This is lovely indeed, but not how I imagined my wedding night!

Yes, Louis and I are wed, but he is camped farther up the road. It is all to fool Father's enemies, until we can reach the fortress of Taillebourg, a few days north of here. Until we are out of the lands of Angoulême, the fleur-de-lis flags will be rolled up and hidden. Bandits of course know that this is the royal caravan, but they won't be able to spot where the prince, or I, are sleeping.

Petra and I are exhausted and hungry. Neither of us ate much at the banquet. Our supper this evening was apricots, bread, and cold water from the river. I must close my eyes for a moment to rest, so will write later . . . .

Near midnight

To continue about our wedding: After the ties on my dress were laced up, I made my way down the stairs with Petra. Our gowns trailed behind us, swishing over the stones. In the courtyard Clotaire the Strong helped me mount my horse, then my sister hers. Prince Louis rode next to me, a royal blue robe over his shoulders. We smiled at the sight of each other; his eyes beamed with pride. Truly, he looked handsome. Under the blazing sun we rode through the streets; villagers cheered and threw flowers. The fronts of their houses were pretty with decorations, and already they were drinking from the barrels of wine that had been rolled out from our cellars.

Trumpeters in blue-and-gold tunics heralded our arrival; church bells rang. Finally we entered the cool church. Standing inside were hundreds of nobles and ladies in elegant dress. They all turned to watch as Louis and I walked up to the altar. Narrow windows above the rafters drew up smoke from the many candles and much incense.

Archbishop du Loroux looked the most relieved I'd ever seen him. After we said our vows, we bent our heads forward so that he could place golden crowns on our heads. We were now formally Duke and Duchess of Aquitaine. Next week when we arrive in my old home, we will be crowned Count and Countess of Poitou. I do not know if there will be a ceremony in Paris to announce that I am also Princess Royal of France.

As we left the church, now man and wife, Louis held up my hand before the waiting crowd and cried, "Eat, drink, and be merry!" People shouted their congratulations and burst into song as we made our way back to Ombrière palace.

The banquet was more splendid than all the others I could recall. There were roasted swans and peacocks, geese and cranes, cinnamon tarts and rice baked in almond milk. The lobster set before me was as plump as a cat, but I pushed it away. I was too nervous to eat. Even the oysters didn't tempt me. Wine I do love, but I turned my cup upside down. I did not want to be groggy.

At last Louis nudged me under the table with his foot. <u>Time to leave.</u>

Our thousand guests were too drunk to notice that he

and I quickly left the great hall. I hurried up to my apartment. In minutes I had thrown off my gown and changed into a plain dress with a brown kirtle. Petra did the same.

Grandmère squeezed us good-bye, then urged us away. "Hurry now, hurry," she cried. Oh, our tears!

Madame, Petra, I, and six of our ladies were escorted to the river, where a boat waited to ferry us across. I was startled to see no trace of the royal camp. All had been packed hours earlier and moved north. At least one hundred knights on horseback were now waiting to escort us along a river toward Saintes. This was to avoid the road going through Angoulême and past the castles of Father's enemies.

Alas, my candle is nearly out . . . more tomorrow.

July 26th, traveling

The heat smothers us, but we must keep moving along this dusty road. We slept only a few hours last night. Long before dawn, when only starlight lit the way, we were roused to continue north. Now we are camped again. My dress is dirty, for I have worn it since yesterday afternoon. I washed my hands in the river, but was hurried into a tent for safety before I could splash my face.

The campfire outside casts shadows against the sides of

our tent, silhouetting the soldiers pacing. So many thoughts come to mind. It is hard to believe I am married! The day was a blur, perhaps because of the heat, but also I was distracted, knowing there were troublemakers who might try to kidnap me. Just moments ago, Abbot Suger told us he is still worried about an ambush. He hopes we reach the safety of Taillebourg by tomorrow.

July 27th
Taillebourg Castle

We crossed the drawbridge late this morning and entered a protected courtyard. I have just a few minutes to write before Petra and I go down to the great hall to meet our hosts. Tonight she will sleep by herself because Louis and I have been given a private suite. I have not seen my husband since our wedding banquet! He must have arrived here safely, because the royal flags are flying from the main turret.

Out the arrow slit we can see that the king's army has camped on the other side of the moat. This castle belongs to Geoffrey de Rançon, one of Father's most loyal lords. I remember coming here when I was younger, on one of Father's ducal visits. We will stay overnight, to rest the horses and ourselves.

After we arrived, Petra and I climbed the stairs to walk along the ramparts, from tower to tower. It felt good to stretch our legs. The countryside is green and lovely, just as I remembered. The Charente River winds through grassy fields toward the sea. I looked northeast, in the direction of Poitiers. We'll be there in a few days, and I can show Louis the secret rock where Petra and I hid so many afternoons.

Five months ago when we left Poitiers, I never dreamed that on our return Father would not be with us. Nor that I would be married and going to Paris. Suddenly I miss Grandmère! She's staying in Bordeaux to help the archbishop finalize Father's affairs, then will come to be with me. I don't want anything to happen to her, so I will send chevaliers as an escort. Perhaps the falconer will come with her, to bring Snow-Jer and our other birds. He is staying at Talmont-by-the-Sea until autumn.

I would also like Marcabru to join our royal court.

Evening, late

Louis was so happy to see me, he took my hand and pressed it to his cheek. The hall was grand with tapestries hanging along the walls, and high above there were windows to let in light. We walked the length of the room, my sister behind us, to the applause of the nobles who had come to congratulate us. I felt such relief knowing we wouldn't have to rush away in the middle of our banquet. This fortress is well protected and far from Angoulême.

In a ceremony honoring our marriage, I was surprised by several of my knights who had followed our caravan. They were dressed in full armor with tunics embroidered with the Aquitaine coat of arms. Clotaire the Strong came before me and kneeled.

"M'lady Eleanor," he said. He repeated his oath of fealty that he had given last year. The others did the same. I was touched by their loyalty and comforted knowing that Petra and I would not be completely alone in our new home.

August 1st
Poitiers

Finally we've reached my ancestral home! How good it feels to be back amid familiar rooms and servants. I have washed and put on a fresh dress; so has Petra. My husband is at the stables, getting ready to ride to Talmont-by-the-Sea. About that later.

First, to tell of our return. What joy it was when at long last I finally saw the city gates. The heat felt unbearable until we neared the river and its woodsy path. Petra and I wanted to run ahead as we would do when we were younger, but we held ourselves back. Everywhere we looked, villagers were hurrying from the fields and their cottages to line the road. They met our caravan with cheers and song. Children waved colorful banners. I was touched by the flowers thrown toward me and the cries of "Lady Eleanor!" I saw tears on the faces of grandmothers. Their welcome melted my heart.

As soon as we stepped into our cool, shaded courtyard, I did run. Louis followed, holding my hand as I led him upstairs. In the treasure room I opened the ducal chest that father had said would be mine when I married. I gave Louis a ring, a silver hourglass, and an ebony box filled with gold coins, to show him how happy I was. Then, in full view of the servants, he pulled me into his arms and kissed me! I nearly fainted with surprise.

I am famished. Supper is in a few minutes. More later.

August 9th

Yesterday in the Poitiers cathederal, among hundreds of loyal subjects, Louis and I were declared Count and Countess of Poitou. It was a dazzling ceremony, performed by the proud, white-haired abbot, Suger. But later, when my maids were removing the robe from my shoulders, I burst into tears. I don't know why. When Petra saw this, <u>she</u> started to cry. So there we were in a puddle, our maids murmuring comforting words. They said that for a girl of fifteen, I have experienced much sorrow and joy.

Madame put her arms around me. "Tears are to be expected, my dear," she said.

Louis is waiting. There's a banquet downstairs in the great hall, and already the sounds of music and laughter are filling the corridors. I will try to write more tomorrow.

Next morning

Louis and a few dozen chevaliers rode off this morning before sunrise. I miss him already! This is what happened:

A courier brought news about the baron of Lezay. The reason he was not here yesterday to swear fealty to us is because he and his men have seized our castle at Talmont! He took Snow-Jer from the falconer and stole our other birds. I told Abbot Suger that we cannot let this insult pass. That is why my husband, the new duke of Aquitaine, is on his way there.

I'm certain that when Lezay sees the royal flags and so

many knights in armor, he will surrender. It will be the last time he tries to cause trouble in Aquitaine.

August 12th

A messenger just came through the gates, his horse covered with foam from riding so hard. Petra and I ran into the courtyard to hear the news.

And what terrible news! While on the road, my husband's chevaliers were so suffering from the heat that they removed their chain mail and helmets and sent everything ahead on a baggage cart. They misunderstood the danger, for as soon as they neared the ocean, Lezay captured some of them and is now holding them hostage. He had hoped to take Prince Louis for ransom. How dare he! Doesn't he know he has defied the king's army?

I'm worried about my husband. He told me that he has never used a sword except in pageantry and that the most risky thing he's ever done is climb a tree. He is not ready for battle. Why did his men treat this journey as if they were going on a holiday?

My sister has been my calm companion. In the chapel she knelt beside me to pray, the familiar pigeons cooing overhead.

The moon is rising on this hot summer night. From the roof we watch the road, hoping to see torchlight coming this way.

Some days later

I woke to Abbot Suger's voice. "Madame la duchesse?"

Petra and I had fallen asleep in our favorite alcove. I sat up. "Yes?"

"Your husband is alive," he said. "His men have killed Lezay's bandits, all except a few who escaped to the sea through an underground passage. It is believed they drowned."

I felt relief, knowing Louis was safe, and excited to think of him bravely saving my castle.

But my heart sank at what we heard next.

Baron William of Lezay was captured by our chevaliers and made to lie in the dirt. While they held him down, his arms stretched out, someone chopped off his hands with an ax.

That someone was a boy who had never before used a weapon.

Louis.

This baron will never try to bother the prince again. Nor will he be able to fondle another maiden.

Traveling again

We are on our way to Paris, the king's five hundred chevaliers escorting us. Also with us is my household from Poitiers, nearly two dozen loyal servants who've known me since childhood. When I told Abbot Suger that they were coming, too, he begged me to be reasonable.

"Please, Madame," he said, "it is too much of an extravagance. The king is going to be upset by the extra costs." But Louis dismissed the abbot, telling him I could have anything I want. So our caravan is slowly moving north.

Because of the extreme heat, Petra and I are traveling in a shaded coach. My diary is on my lap, but the roughness of the road has made the ink smear in places. Louis is riding alongside us. He took off his armor <u>and</u> his shirt to keep cool.

We have not yet talked about Talmont.

The road curves ahead. I can see dust from riders coming this way. Some of our knights are galloping up to them to see if it is safe for us to proceed. I will write more when there is not so much commotion.

Next evening

We are camped alongside a river. Smoke from our cooking fires drifts up through the trees, reminding me of my fierce hunger. I have not eaten since last night. The events of yesterday have left me in such shock that I don't know where to begin. . . .

My coach drew to a stop when the knights ahead of us began shouting. I could not hear them, but they seemed to be celebrating. Abbot Suger and several advisers rode up to us, dismounted, then bowed down to my husband. I lifted my skirt to step out of the carriage, for I wanted to hear what the abbot would say.

His words to Louis left me speechless. He said, "I am sorry to deliver this news to you, Highness, but your father the king is dead. You are now king of France." Then the abbot turned to me and made a low, sweeping bow.

"Queen Eleanor," he said, "I am at your service."

I am queen?

Now I'm sitting in the shade, Petra at my side, wondering what will happen next. The courier told us that Louis the Fat died on August 1, from diarrhea and "summer fevers." I read back in this diary . . . August 1 was the day we arrived in Poitiers. Would Father believe his daughter would become queen after one week of marriage? I cannot.

Louis is standing alone on the riverbank, staring into the water. I will go comfort him, for I remember well the loss of my own father. Then I will give thought to Paris.

I am queen, and as queen there is much to be done.

Epilogue

When Eleanor arrived in Poitiers on August 1, 1137, she had no way of knowing that in Paris, at that very moment, her father-in-law the king lay dying of dysentery. He was so fat that he could not get out of bed to use the garderobe, so his room smelled like a privy. At his request, his attendants rolled him onto the floor, then onto a carpet sprinkled with ashes in the shape of a cross. He stretched out his arms on this "cross" and died, leaving his son, Louis, king of his newly expanded realm.

As queen of France, fifteen-year-old Eleanor found life in Paris difficult. The royal palace was on the Île-de-France, an almond-shaped island in the middle of the Seine, and was even colder and draftier than her castles in the south of France. Louis was not the gallant knight she'd hoped for. In fact, he resumed his studies and meditations at the church of Notre Dame. Though he was king of France, he preferred the life of a monk. He dressed simply, sang in the monastic choir, and fasted every Friday on bread and water. Eleanor missed the troubadours and the dancing, feasting, and merrymaking that were common in Aquitaine. Her closest companion was her sister, Petronilla.

Louis and Eleanor's marriage was not a happy one. Only when Louis agreed to lead a crusade to the Holy Lands near Jerusalem did Eleanor have hope for him. A determined and persistent woman, she demanded to accompany him. Finally, Louis agreed, and in June of 1147 he turned over the safekeeping of his kingdom to Abbot Suger, so that he and his wife could travel, hoping to reclaim the Holy Land and revive their marriage.

The amount of personal luggage Eleanor took was staggering. A long line of wagons carried trunks filled with gowns, jewels, cosmetics, and furs. Household items included tents, mattresses, rugs, silver washbasins, and goblets. Dozens of noblewomen, knights from Aquitaine, minstrels, and troubadours were her traveling companions.

The journey lasted two and a half years, during which time the danger and stress further eroded Eleanor's relationship with Louis. The expedition was such a disaster that the royal couple barely escaped with their lives. When they returned to Paris, Eleanor had their marriage annulled; Louis took custody of their daughters, Marie and Alix.

In 1152, eight weeks after her marriage to Louis ended, Eleanor wed Henry of Anjou, a great-grandson of William the Conqueror. She was thirty, and though Henry was only nineteen, he already had laid claim to the throne of England through his mother, Matilda. Eleanor, of course, still controlled Aquitaine. It was a powerful political union that also produced eight children.

As a skillful military leader, Henry defeated King Stephen of England and was named his successor. A few years later Henry was crowned king when Stephen died suddenly.

Henry, now Henry II, and Eleanor set about ruling England. It was a peaceful time in Britain and in their marriage. This period of several years was among Eleanor's happiest. But tragedy struck soon.

The royal couple's first child, William, died at the age of two. But Eleanor was to have several more sons and potential heirs to the throne. This led to much turmoil within the royal family for the rest of her life. Because of her intrigues, Henry put Eleanor in prison.

Their sons were Henry, Richard, Geoffrey, and John. Eleanor favored Richard above all, and they all plotted to seize power. Young Henry and Geoffrey revolted against their father, unsuccessfully, and met untimely deaths. Richard ("the Lionheart") and John joined French forces and were successful. Henry II died soon thereafter, perhaps in no small measure from parental grief, and Richard became king in 1189. Eleanor, who had been imprisoned for sixteen years, was finally freed at age sixty-seven. She had such a great sense of pageantry that she carefully planned Richard's coronation ceremony. Some of these procedures for crowning an English monarch are still used today.

But her intrigues weren't over. She fought fiercely for John's right to claim the throne after Richard's death, and, at age eighty, journeyed to her homeland to prevent the French from defeating John and seizing her beloved Aquitaine. Making her headquarters in a castle, she was surrounded by the French and in danger of being captured. Only John's timely arrival with a small army saved her and what remained of their vast kingdom.

The last days of Eleanor's life are blank. For an educated woman, she left few records. Some accounts say she was consecrated as a nun in 1202 and died two years later in Fontevrault abbey, just north of Poitiers, France. Her tomb can be seen there today, placed between that of her second husband, Henry II, and her beloved son, Richard the Lionheart. One of her descendants is the present Queen Elizabeth of England.

Of Petronilla, it is said that she was beautiful and charm-ing. She fell in love with Count Ralph of Vermandois, who was at least thirty years older than she, but unfortu-nately he was already married. Since Eleanor wanted her sister to be happy, she arranged to have the count's mar-riage annulled. When Pope Innocent learned of this arrangement and that Ralph and Petronilla had wed, he excommunicated them. They had a son, who later died of leprosy, and two daughters.

Life in France,
1136

𝕳𝖎𝖘𝖙𝖔𝖗𝖎𝖈𝖆𝖑 𝕹𝖔𝖙𝖊

Eleanor of Aquitaine became the queen of France when she was fifteen years old, and for the next sixty-seven years she was to remain a queen, first of France, and then of England. By all accounts she was intelligent and beautiful, but a true likeness of her does not exist. That she was headstrong and spoiled is undisputed. She liked clothes and jewelry, music and dance, and had a carefree and undisciplined childhood. Her health was vigorous, for she gave birth to ten children, nine of whom lived to adulthood. Eleanor's death at the age of eighty-two is remarkable, considering that the average life span for someone in the Middle Ages was roughly half that.

The date of her birth is not known for certain, but it is believed to be 1122. Born to a family of wealth and privilege, she was the eldest daughter of William X, duke of Aquitaine. She had a younger sister, Petronilla, and a brother, William Aigret. When Eleanor was eight, both young William and her mother died, just a few months apart. These tragic events shaped Eleanor's life in both personal and political ways.

Unless Eleanor's father remarried and produced a male heir, she would be in line to inherit Aquitaine, a vast territory from the Loire to the Pyrenees, larger than the kingdom of France. But when Eleanor was fifteen, her father died unexpectedly while on a religious pilgrimage to Spain. This made her the most eligible girl in all of Europe and set into motion her immediate betrothal to the king's son, Louis the Younger. One week after their marriage, however, another untimely death — the king's — made her husband Louis VII, the new king. He was sixteen, one year older than she was.

Some items of interest during the time of Eleanor's life are worth noting:

It was highly unusual for girls, even of Eleanor's rank, to be as carefully educated as she was. At a young age girls were shown how to embroider, sew, spin, weave, and sing. They also learned falconry and horseback riding, along with games of checkers, backgammon, and chess. Daughters of noble families were expected to be well mannered and to carry on family titles by having children; sons were instructed in knighthood. One of the reasons girls were rarely taught to read and write was that it was believed they would waste time writing love letters and daydreaming, all of which might lead to promiscuity.

Eleanor could read French and Latin, and was so fond of romantic literature that she was the patron of writers and poets in her later life. It is thought that she studied the basics of mathematics and enough astronomy to identify the constellations.

Langue d'oc, or Provençal, was Eleanor's mother tongue, a French dialect, spoken in Aquitaine, which came from the language spoken by early Roman invaders. She probably also spoke langue d'oeil, the dialect used north of the Loire River, the ancestor of modern French.

The legends of King Arthur were told in stories, songs, and poems, often by storytellers and troubadours who entertained the noble families. Both Eleanor and King Henry were fascinated by these tales, which they had heard from childhood; one of their grandsons was even named Arthur. There are differing opinions as to when the doomed romance of Queen Guinevere and Lancelot was first told. The legends say that they and King Arthur lived during the sixth century, so it is entirely possible that these stories were handed down in the oral tradition long before they appeared in writing. The earliest written accounts seem to have been by Geoffrey of Monmouth around 1135, and the Round Table story was introduced later in the same century by Robert Wace.

Some meals from the twelfth century are still enjoyed today: coq au vin, bouillabaisse, beef bourguignonne, and omelettes. Popular sweets were gingerbread, dried fruit, macaroons, waffles, and tarts. Since forks hadn't yet been invented, the only utensils used at meals were spoons and knives; drinks were cider or ale and wine spiced with cloves.

During the 1130s, Paris had a population of about 200,000 and a stimulating intellectual climate. Students came from all over Europe to attend the schools famous for debate and scholarship. Eleanor may have listened to lectures given by the renowned scholar Peter Abelard, who boasted that noble ladies flocked to his lectures. By then his ill-fated love affair with Héloïse and his monastic vow of chastity were already legend. These years of intellectual revival are now referred to as the Twelfth-Century Renaissance. In 1163, the construction of Notre Dame cathedral began while Louis VII was king.

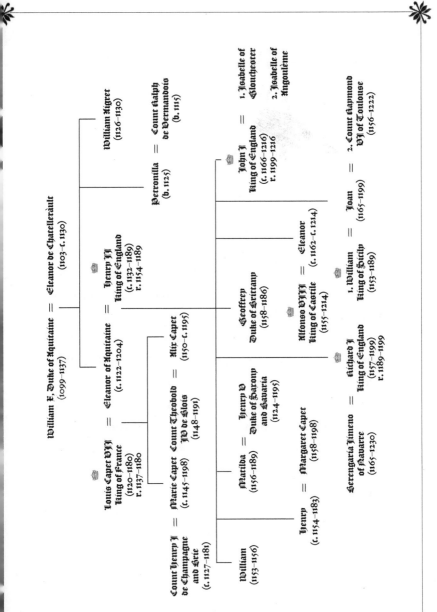

The Capet–Plantagenet Family Tree

A formidable alliance was created on July 25, 1137, with the marriage of fifteen-year-old Eleanor of Aquitaine and sixteen-year-old Louis VII of Paris, France. Young Eleanor brought to the union one quarter of all the land of France — territories she'd inherited from her father William, duke of Aquitaine, which was more land than Louis's father, King Louis VI of France, ever owned. The marriage, however, ended in annulment in 1152. Weeks later, Eleanor wed Henry Plantagenet, count of Anjou (who two years later became King Henry II of England), and transferred her vast holdings to him. Coupled with his English holdings, these made Henry a more powerful force than Louis VII, causing a long and bitter rivalry between the two men. Ten children in total were produced from the two marriages. The family tree chart illustrates the lineage beginning with Eleanor's father, William X, duke of Aquitaine. Dates of birth and death (when available) are noted. The crown symbol indicates those who ruled. Double lines represent marriages; single lines indicate parentage.

William X, duke of Aquitaine: Father of Eleanor of Aquitaine and Petronilla; also known as Count William of Poitiers, and son of William the Conqueror, the most famous troubador of his time. Count William died from food poisoning while on a pilgrimage to Spain in 1137.

Eleanor de Chatellerault: Wife of Count William de Poitiers; mother of Eleanor of Aquitaine, Petronilla, and William Aigret. She died in 1130 when Eleanor was just eight years old.

Children of Count William X, duke of Aquitaine and Eleanor de Chatellerault

Eleanor of Aquitaine: Eldest daughter of William X, duke of Aquitaine. With her marriage to Louis VII, she became queen of France (1137-1152). At age thirty, she married nineteen-year-old Henry Plantagenet and became queen of England (1154-1204) when he succeeded to the British throne as King Henry II of England. Together the two marriages produced ten children, two of whom would become kings of England. She spent her last days at the abbey in Fontevrault, France, where she died on April 1, 1204.

Petronilla: Second daughter of William X, duke of Aquitaine; sister of Eleanor. Her marriage to Count Ralph de Vermandois produced three children.

William Aigret: Third child of William X, duke of Aquitaine; brother of Eleanor and Petronilla. He died in the year 1130 when he was only four years old.

Eleanor's Husbands

Louis Capet VII: Son of King Louis VI (Louis the Fat) of France; first husband of Eleanor of Aquitaine. Their marriage lasted for fifteen years, during which Eleanor bore two daughters, Marie and Alix.

Henry II: Second husband of Eleanor of Aquitaine; great-grandson of William the Conqueror, who was Eleanor's grandfather. Together, Eleanor and Henry had eight children: three daughters and five sons, two of whom — Richard (Richard the Lionheart) and John — rose to the British crown. Henry II died in Chinon, France, on July 6, 1189.

Children of Eleanor of Aquitaine

Marie Capet: Countess of Champagne; firstborn daughter of Eleanor and Louis VII. She was married to Count Henry I of Champagne and Brie, with whom she had four children.

Alix Capet: Second daughter of Eleanor and Louis VII. She became the wife of Count Theobald IV de Blois.

William Plantagenet: Firstborn son of Eleanor and Henry II. He died at three years old.

Henry Plantagenet: Eleanor's fourth child; second born to her and Henry II. He married Margaret Capet of France, and they had one son, John.

Matilda Plantagenet: Also known as Maud, Eleanor's fifth child; third child born to her and Henry II. She was the wife of Duke Henry V of Saxony and Bavaria, and, like her mother, she also had ten children.

Richard I: Eleanor's sixth child; the fourth born to her and Henry II. His mother's favorite son, he succeeded his father and ruled England for ten years as King Richard I (Richard the Lionheart). Wounded by an arrow, he died in Aquitaine, France, in April 1199.

Geoffrey Plantagenet: Seventh child of Eleanor; fifth child born to her and Henry II. Geoffrey held the title of duke of Brittany.

Eleanor Plantagenet: Her mother's namesake and eighth child; the sixth child with Henry II. She married King Alfonso VIII of Castile, with whom she had twelve children.

Joan Plantagenet: Ninth child of Eleanor; seventh child with Henry II. Her first husband was King William of Sicily, and her second was Count Raymond VI of Toulouse. Together, the two marriages produced four children.

John Plantagenet: Eleanor's fifth son and tenth child; upon his brother Richard's death, he succeeded him as king of England and ruled as John Lackland from 1199 until his death in 1216.

A steel engraving of Eleanor of Aquitaine from the nineteenth century. This image is a representation of Eleanor when she was married to King Henry II of England.

Above is an engraving of Eleanor's first husband, King Louis VII of France. Louis married Eleanor at age fifteen, shortly after the death of her father. Below is an engraving of Louis's father, King Louis Capet VI, also known as Louis the Fat. He ruled France from 1108 until his death in 1137. Considered an effective ruler, he spent most of his reign immersed in various war efforts.

Portrait of Henry II, second husband of Eleanor of Aquitaine, who reigned as king of England from 1154 to 1189.

A portrait of Richard the Lionheart, Eleanor's favorite son. Her fourth child with Henry, Richard reigned as king of England from 1189 to 1199.

A fifteenth–century painting depicting farmers gathering the harvest outside of the château de Poitiers in France. Eleanor spent much of her childhood in this expansive castle.

This crystal vase, on exhibit at the Louvre Museum in Paris, was a gift from Eleanor to Louis VII after they married. It is said to be the last surviving authentic artifact having belonged to the royal couple.

Standard protective uniforms of French knights in the Middle Ages. Although there are variations in costume, most soldiers wore chain mail and a helmet and carried an armored shield, axe or spear, and sword.

Illustration of knights from the Middle Ages engaging in a jousting tournament. These tournaments were a form of entertainment for the royal court.

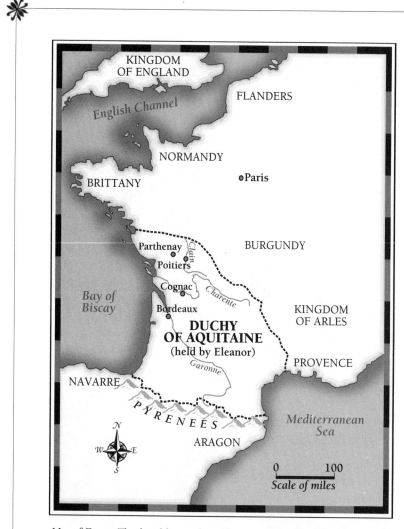

Map of France. The dotted lines indicate the vast territory controlled by Eleanor of Aquitaine, extending from Parthenay to the Pyrenees Mountains.

A modern photograph of Fontevrault abbey church. Declared a sacred structure in 1109, the abbey's church is the burial place of the early Plantagenet kings of England and the final resting place of Eleanor of Aquitaine.

Effigy of Eleanor of Aquitaine. Constructed in the thirteenth century, the sculptured tomb depicts Eleanor holding a book, which represents her intelligence and love of learning. Her effigy lies between those of Henry II and their son Richard I.

Glossary of Characters

[*indicates fictional character]

Anacletus — the antipope; an ambitious cardinal who claimed papal authority from 1130 to 1138.

Arthur — hero of many medieval legends; believed to have ruled the Britons in the sixth century.

*Barber — viscount in Aquitaine, disloyal to Duke William X.

Bernard Abbé — [1090–1153] a monk who founded the abbey of Clairvaux and was among the founders of the Cistercian Order; was the most admired churchman of the twelfth century, regarded as a saint in his lifetime, and canonized after his death.

*Brother Jean-Pierre — one of the monks in Poitiers.

*Clotaire the Strong — Eleanor's favorite knight.

Eleanor — [ca. 1122–1204] daughter of Duke William X of Aquitaine; became queen of France in 1137 at the age of fifteen, then queen of England in 1154. She had ten children. Two of her sons became kings of England: Richard the Lionheart [1157–1199] and John [1166–1216].

Emma — daughter of Viscount Aymar of Limoges; was betrothed to Eleanor's father but was abducted by, and forced to marry, Count William of Angoulême.

Geoffrey de Rançon — lord of Taillebourg, one of Duke William X's most loyal vassals.

Geoffrey du Loroux — archbishop of Bordeaux; performed the marriage ceremony for Eleanor and Louis on July 25, 1137.

Geoffrey "the Handsome" Plantagenet of Anjou — [1113–1151] count who invited Duke William X to help him invade Normandy in 1136. His wife was Matilda, daughter of King Henry I of England; their son, Henry II, married Eleanor in 1152.

*Grandmère — Eleanor's grandmother.

Guinevere — sixth-century queen; wife of King Arthur.

Innocent II — pope from 1130 to 1143.

Lancelot — one of the knights in the medieval legend of King Arthur.

Louis the Fat — [1081–1137] King Louis Capet VI of France.

Louis the Younger — [ca. 1120–1180] Prince Louis Capet

(later King Louis VII) of France; Eleanor's first husband; became king upon his father's death on August 1, 1137.

*Madame — Eleanor's chief lady-in-waiting.

Marcabru — one of the favorite troubadours patronized by Duke William X.

Petronilla ("Petra") — [ca. 1125–?] Eleanor's younger sister.

Suger — [1081–1151] abbot of Saint-Denis and royal counselor to King Louis the Fat; he was his lifelong confidant and chief administrator; performed the ceremony of investiture for Louis the Younger and Eleanor as Count and Countess of Poitou.

William Aigret ("Willie") — [ca. 1126–1130] Eleanor's younger brother.

William of Angoulême — count who kidnapped Duke William X's intended bride, Emma.

William of Lezay — baron and castellan of Talmont-by-the-Sea; disloyal to Duke William X.

William IX — [1071–1126] duke of Aquitaine; known as the first troubadour, famous for writing erotic and blasphemous poetry.

William X — [1099–1137] duke of Aquitaine; Eleanor's father.

William and Joscelin — illegitimate sons of Duke William X; Eleanor's half brothers.

About the Author

Kristiana Gregory says about writing *Eleanor: Crown Jewel of Aquitaine, France, 1136:* "It was a lot of fun imagining a fourteen-year-old girl living during the Middle Ages. I love teenagers and I love medieval history. Of course it was a great help traveling to France with a group of American high school students, and then touring the Aquitaine country with them. I'm convinced many of the concerns and interests kids have today are similar to those of eight centuries ago: friendship, parental love, curiosity about their future, yearnings for adventure and, of course, cool clothes."

On a subsequent trip to Paris, Ms. Gregory explored the Louvre Museum, in search of what is believed to be the only surviving artifact owned by Eleanor. After some interesting conversations in fractured French and several wrong turns, Ms. Gregory finally found the exhibit: a crystal vase about sixteen inches tall, encrusted with jewels. "It was beautiful," she says. "Most of the gems were each about the size of my thumbnail, in an array of blues and violets, set into silver." It is said that Eleanor was fifteen and newly married to King Louis VII when she gave the vase to him. The Latin inscription on its base states that after she presented it to Louis, he gave it to Abbot Suger, who then donated it to the Abbey of Saint-Denis in Paris.

Kristiana Gregory's other Royal Diary is *Cleopatra VII, Daughter of the Nile: Egypt, 57 B.C.*, which was made into a movie for the HBO Family Channel. Her most recent Dear America title is *Seeds of Hope: The Gold Rush Diary of Susanna Fairchild, California Territory, 1849,* named Best Book of the Year by Oppenheim Toy Portfolio. Her first book, *Jenny of the Tetons,* won the Golden Kite Award for Fiction from the Society of Children's Book Writers and Illustrators.

She lives in Boise, Idaho, with her family.

Acknowledgments

Much appreciation to Father John F. Donoghue, Diocese of Boise, Idaho, for his colorful explanations and insights into the twelfth-century Roman Catholic Church; and to Annie Anderson, a good friend and careful reader.

Cover painting by Tim O'Brien

Page 171: Engraving of Eleanor of Aquitaine, Mary Evans Picture Library, London.

Page 172 (top): Engraving of King Louis VII, Mary Evans Picture Library, London.

Page 172 (bottom): Engraving of King Louis VI, Mary Evans Picture Library, London.

Page 173: Portrait of Henry II, North Wind Picture Archives, Alfred, Maine.

Page 174: Portrait of Richard I, Mary Evans Picture Library, London.

Page 175: Château de Poitiers, Mary Evans Picture Library, London.

Page 176: Crystal vase, Kristiana Gregory.

Page 177 (top): French knights, The Art Archive/Musée des Arts Décoratifs Paris/Dagli Orti (A).

Page 177 (bottom): Knights jousting, North Wind Picture Archives, Alfred, Maine.

Page 178: Map of France, James McMahon.

Page 179: Fontevrault Abbey, Adam Woolfitt/CORBIS.

Page 180: Eleanor's effigy, Erich Lessing/Art Resource, New York, New York.

Other books in The Royal Diaries series

ELIZABETH I
Red Rose of the House of Tudor
by Kathryn Lasky

CLEOPATRA VII
Daughter of the Nile
by Kristiana Gregory

ISABEL
Jewel of Castilla
by Carolyn Meyer

MARIE ANTOINETTE
Princess of Versailles
by Kathryn Lasky

ANASTASIA
The Last Grand Duchess
by Carolyn Meyer

NZINGHA
Warrior Queen of Matamba
by Patricia C. McKissack

KAIULANI
The People's Princess
by Ellen Emerson White

With love to my favorite research companions, my patient sons, Greg and Cody.

While the Royal Diaries are based on real royal figures
and actual historical events, some situations and people in
this book are fictional, created by the author.

Library of Congress Cataloging-in-Publication Data
Gregory, Kristiana.
Eleanor of Aquitaine / by Kristiana Gregory.
p. cm. — (The royal diaries)
Summary: The diary of Eleanor, first daughter of the duke of Aquitaine,
from 1136 until 1137, when at age fifteen she becomes queen of France.
Includes historical notes on her later life.
ISBN 0-439-16484-2
1. Eleanor of Aquitaine, Queen, consort of Henry II, King of England,
1122?–1204 — Childhood and youth — Juvenile fiction. 2. France —
History — Louis VII, 1137–1180 — Juvenile fiction. [1. Eleanor of Aquitaine,
Queen, consort of Henry II, King of England, 1122?–1204 — Childhood
and youth — Fiction. 2. France — History — Louis VII, 1137–1180 —
Fiction. 3. Kings, queens, rulers, etc. — Fiction. 4. Diaries — Fiction.]
I. Title. II. Series.
PZ7.G8619 El 2002
[Fic] — dc21   2001057628

10 9 8 7 6 5 4 3 2 1   02 03 04 05 06

The text type in this book was set in Augereau.
The display type was set in Aquitaine Initials.
Book design by Elizabeth B. Parisi

Printed in the U.S.A.   23
First printing, September 2002